Perseverance

Perseverance

To Your Health

Maureen McIntyre

Maureen McIntyre

To order additional copies of this book, contact:
Xlibris LLC
1-888-795-4274
www.Xlibris.com
Orders@Xlibris.com
139755

CONTENTS

DEDICATION

This book is dedicated to my best friend Sal and my son, Ron, for always being there for me.

Thanks also goes to my sister, Sandra, for her excellent editing skills.

AUTHOR'S REMARKS

This book was written as a fictitious romance novel. Characters and storyline are purely fictional.

The medical part of this book, however, is factual in all respects. The condition of NPH, the symptoms, tests and treatments are real and true.

PROLOGUE

"Well, my divorce is final today."

Eighteen months ago Joe, her husband of twenty-five years, and Vicki were in the Bahamas relaxing on lovely striped cotton lounge chairs on the beach. The light brown sand looked very fine and tempting to walk on. As they sat there enjoying the wonderful warm day, the waves on the beautiful azure ocean kissed the shore and made such a relaxing sound.

Vicki closed her eyes and thought about how her life was with Joe and their twenty-three year old son, Charlie. She was so happy to be basking in the warm sun and away from all the pressures of work.

When their week was finished, they returned home and back to work. At the beginning of their work week, Joe said:

"Sweetheart, how about meeting me for lunch on Friday at our favourite bistro at twelve thirty and if we can both book off Friday afternoon, we can start our weekend early?"

"I would love that Joe, thanks. You have such wonderful ideas sometimes and we both need to take some time off to rest from our busy jobs."

Her confusion came, she thought, because she was so busy at work. On Thursday she rushed out the door at noon, thinking it was Friday and hurried to the restaurant for her date with Joe. As she entered the Bistro the most shocking scene hit her squarely in the face.

"Could that be Joe?"

"Who is he with?"

"I think I recognize her. Oh Yes!" It was his young secretary.

They were holding hands across the table. Vicki hid behind a Japanese Red Maple that was in the entrance area. She wanted to watch for a few minutes. She really wished she wasn't watching because what she saw would stay with her forever.

Joe and his home-wrecking secretary leaned across the table and gave each other a very passionate looking kiss.

Vicki turned and ran out of the restaurant, tears streaming down her face. She ran the three blocks to their home wondering how he could do such a cruel thing to her when he knew she was on her way to meet him for lunch.

As Vicki ran with tears still pouring from her eyes, she passed a coffee shop. She happened to see a sign that had been placed outside the shop and it read:

THURSDAY SPECIAL
Coffee and blueberry muffin
$3.50

"Oh no!"

In all her confusion, Vicki had mixed up the days. She thought it was Friday when it actually was only Thursday. Even though Vicki was extremely busy at work, she was always very organized. This mix-up was not a normal occurrence for her.

When Joe returned home, they had a huge fight. He tried to convince her that it was just a business lunch but she had seen enough to know that this was a lie.

Since this was not the first time Joe had cheated, Vicki said: "Joe, I want a divorce."

CHAPTER 1

VICKI

Victoria Burke had recently been promoted to her dream job as a buyer for a large fashion house, Great Fashion Choice (GFC), in Toronto. She was recently divorced from her husband, Joe. At fifty years of age she was worried she may never find another man. As she entered her upscale condo, she greeted the doorman, Alfred.

"Good morning Alfred, lovely day today."

Alfred had been doorman at this building since it was built five years ago. He was very helpful and liked to carry packages for the single ladies. Perhaps he fancied himself as some kind of ladies' man?

Vicki took the elevator to her third floor suite. It was tastefully decorated with a beautiful white leather couch and chair and occasional chairs in beige silk with a touch of burnt orange in the fabric. The fireplace mantle was adorned with expensive figurines. On the eighteenth century Tuscan console table were pictures of her twenty five year old son Charles with his new wife Anne, Vicki's sister Margaret with her husband George and their two girls, thirteen year old Emma and ten year old Susan. Maggie was forty five years old and had been happily married for twenty years. There was also a picture of Vicki and Charlie but Joe had been cut from the picture since they divorced one and a half years ago when he started seeing his young secretary.

CHAPTER 2

CHARLES AND ANNE

Nine months earlier

Vicki's only son, twenty four year old Charles, had been dating twenty three year old Anne (Annie) for a few months now. On a Saturday evening they were getting ready to go to Mom's house for dinner. Charles bent down on one knee and Annie was so surprised that her heart started beating very quickly and she felt a little faint. She managed to steady herself and Charlie did not notice, or at least did not let on. Annie was a very petite 5'1" young woman and only one hundred and ten pounds. She was very cute with long red hair and fair skin. She looked like a China doll. Charlie then said:

"Annie, I love you and I want to spend the rest of my life making you happy. Will you marry me?"

Annie was very surprised as they had not even mentioned marriage up to this point but she was thrilled. Annie said:

"I love you too Charlie and I would be honoured to be your wife."

They kissed and hugged for about five minutes, neither one wanting to let go. Charlie had picked out an exquisite solitaire diamond, set in yellow gold and he placed it on Annie's ring finger. It fit perfectly as Charlie had taken a ring from Annie's jewellery box and showed it to the jeweller for sizing.

All the way to Mom's house, in the car, Annie could not take her eyes off her ring. She held her hand out in front of her face and gazed at her sparkling diamond.

"Charlie, I love you and this is the most stunning ring I have ever seen."

Vicki opened the door when Charlie rang from the foyer. As soon as Charlie and Annie entered Vicki's suite, she knew there was a surprise coming as they were grinning like two Cheshire cats.

"Come in and how are you both?" Vicki said.

Immediately she had a hand thrust in front of her face.

"How wonderful, congratulations. I am so happy for you both. Have you thought about a date yet?"

In all the excitement it had not even entered their minds.

"Let's discuss it after dinner and we can choose a venue and a date for the wedding," Annie said.

After they finished a delicious dinner of Pork A L'Orange and a chocolate soufflé for dessert, they retired to the living room with their coffee.

Vicki said: "A June wedding could be lovely and that would give you a few months to plan."

Charlie and Annie agreed. Their church was in downtown Toronto and Charlie said:

"I am a member of the Granite Club and they have great facilities for parties and weddings. I am sure I can make arrangements to have our reception there and it is fairly close to the church."

June the second came very quickly and on the morning of the wedding it was raining. Annie was a little disappointed but the sun came out around noon and all was well again. Annie's friend Debbie told her that if it rained on your wedding day it was considered good luck.

Annie had chosen a beautiful, long, white gown; it had a full skirt and appliques of flowers and petals all the way around. There were rhinestones scattered everywhere and white sequins on each flower. The bodice had a scoop neck and also had appliques from the waist to the neckline with sequins and rhinestones as well. She wore white satin pumps and a single strand of pearls that Charlie had given her at the engagement party thrown by Annie's parents. Annie had asked Maggie's girls, Emma and Susan, to be in the wedding party; Susan was the flower girl and Emma the junior bridesmaid. As Annie was an only child, she had asked two girlfriends, Brenda and Debbie, to be her bridesmaid and maid of honour. Both girls were thrilled to be asked and very happy for Annie and Charlie.

Brenda and Debbie got together and arranged a lovely bridal shower for Annie. It took place at Brenda's house as she was married and had a big house in Pickering, a suburb of Toronto. There were thirty women and girls at the shower and Annie and Charlie received many beautiful gifts such as linens, towels, small kitchen appliances and a lovely set of dishes given to them by Vicki.

Vicki looked gorgeous in a pale blue pant suit and white blouse. She was remembering the shower she had before she married Joe. It had been exciting to have all her friends and relatives giving her gifts and best wishes. She thought Annie must be feeling this same excitement now.

CHAPTER 3

CHARLIE AND ANNIE'S WEDDING

The colours Annie had chosen for her bridesmaids were different shades of mauve ranging from purple and fading to pink.

Vicki, Mother of the Groom, wore a beautiful off-white suit with a pink silk blouse. She looked elegant with her hair styled behind her ears and quite curly. Vicki had chosen long, gold, drop style earrings and a simple gold chain around her neck which sparkled at the neckline of her blouse. She was very nervous today as her ex-husband Joe would be at the wedding. Thank goodness he decided not to bring his girlfriend with him. Vicki and Joe sat together in the church for Charlie and Annie's sake but at the reception they would not be seated together.

Susan wore a light mauve dress with a full skirt. It was just to her ankles so you could see her little, white, ballet slippers. There was a purple sash around her waist that tied in a bow at the back. She was so happy to be part of the wedding. Susan had never even been to a wedding before, so this was a real treat for her.

Emma and Brenda wore dresses in mauve, a shade darker than Susan's. The bridesmaids' dresses were fairly fitted with a scoop neck to match the Bride. These dresses were unique in that they had a separate piece of material that tied around the waist making a long, full skirt with an opening at one side. The dresses could easily be worn again, without the extra skirt, making them knee length. Emma was pleased about this as she had been invited to a birthday party the following month which was being held at Casa Loma in Toronto and the dress was to be formal.

The music started and Susan ventured slowly down the aisle dropping pink rose petals on her way. Right behind Susan was her sister Emma, the Junior Bridesmaid, looking lovely in mauve. Behind Emma was Brenda, a Bridesmaid, also wearing mauve. Debbie, the Maid of Honour, wearing a deep purple, long and form-fitting gown was immediately in front of Annie. Debbie carried pink and white roses with a touch of purple heather. She looked beautiful. Debbie was not married but had been dating Michael for three years now and everyone felt there would be another wedding soon. Both bridesmaids were carrying pink and white daisies. The flowers and bouquets were all expertly arranged by Barb, Vicki's friend and neighbour.

Finally, it was time for the Bride. Everyone stood up as Annie walked down the aisle on her father's arm. She was a little nervous, as most brides are, but she looked gorgeous in her gown and was carrying pink roses with white baby's breath. As soon as she saw Charlie standing at the front of the church waiting for her, she relaxed. Charlie smiled and whispered:

"I love you."

Annie took her place beside Charlie and the service began. When the minister said:

"I now pronounce you husband and wife, you may kiss your Bride," everyone stood up and clapped for the new couple.

All the invited guests gathered at the Granite Club for the receiving line and a wonderful dinner. Debbie gave the first toast to the Bride, followed by Charlie's Best Man, then a short story and toast by Annie's Uncle Alan. After dinner, the Bride and Groom started their first dance and soon others joined the newlyweds on the dance floor. It was a great party and continued until midnight. Annie and Charlie left around ten o'clock to begin their honeymoon. They were leaving in the morning for ten days in Aruba.

CHAPTER 4

MARGARET AND GEORGE

Twenty Two years previously

Twenty two years ago, when she was single, Margaret and three of her girlfriends decided to take a cruise on the Caribbean. This would be the first for all of them.

They went to a travel agent in the mall where they shopped and booked a twelve-day Caribbean cruise leaving from Tampa, Florida. They were all so excited and of course had to shop for cruise wear. Margaret loved shopping and this time it was even more special as they had such a wonderful trip planned.

When the departure date finally came, they met at Pearson Airport to fly to Tampa for a four o'clock departure of their cruise.

The first day they were at sea, and therefore they took advantage of the spa and swimming pool. Their first stop was Ocho Rios, Jamaica where they visited Dunn's River Falls and climbed up the rocks. Margaret fell a couple of times and they were all laughing so hard that all four of them went down. They soon recovered and ventured to the top.

They had another day at sea which was spent in the casino. They had lots of fun and each night they went to the ship's theatre where the staff put on a show. The performers were actually very talented.

The second stop was Curacao and the third stop was Aruba. After another day at sea they were in St. Maarten. They had to take a tender to the island as the ship was too large to dock there. When they got onto the tender there were seats all around the outside. The four girls sat together as they were a bit nervous taking this mode of transportation to the island. Sitting on Margaret's right hand side was a young man who appeared to be travelling alone and they started talking.

"Hi! My name is George. I see you are travelling with your girlfriends. Are you enjoying your trip?"

"Yes, we are having a great time. My name is Margaret. Are you alone?"

"No, I am travelling with a friend but he had too much to drink last night and is sleeping it off today."

"Sorry to hear that but I hope you enjoy your day."

"Thank you, Margaret, and you have a good day too. I am from Canada. Where are you from?"

"I am Canadian too."

He was very nice and polite. When they disembarked they went their separate ways. Margaret and her friends found some stores with beautiful jewellery. Margaret bought a lovely necklace; it was an emerald stone set in sterling silver. She also bought a bottle of Guavaberry Rum. These were her souvenirs of the trip. The next day was the last island stop, St. Thomas, a very picture perfect island with turquoise water and white sandy beaches. The girls spent the day on the beach swimming and sun bathing.

They returned to the ship for two days at sea before the ship was to arrive in Boston to end the cruise. During these two days at sea, Margaret ran into George the young man she had met previously on the tender. They spent an evening together getting to know each other. George asked if he could call her when they got home and she was very flattered and said:

"Yes, of course. I live in Toronto. Where do you live?"

He told Margaret that he lived in Mississauga so they were not too far apart.

A week after the cruise, George did call. They started dating and were married a year later.

CHAPTER 5

VICKI

Early Monday morning as Vicki woke, the sun was shining brightly in her bedroom window. There was a slight breeze and the branches of the trees just past her window were swaying gently.

"What a beautiful day."

"I feel so good today as I am about to make arrangements for a trip to Paris. I cannot wait."

Vicki headed to the shower and also washed her hair. Then, after drying and curling her hair, she chose a brown suit with a cream coloured blouse, brown pumps and matching bag. As she was dressing, she was thinking:

"I must go to the bank today. The bank is only two blocks from home and I can go after work and get some euros for my trip to Paris on Thursday. I am very excited as this is my first buying trip to Paris."

"All the important people in the fashion industry will be there buying their new fashions. There is a fabulous fashion show on Saturday and Joanne, my assistant of three years, is going with me. Joanne is a good assistant and joins me on my buying trips; she has excellent taste and is an asset to me. I must admit I am a little jealous of Joanne; she is a very beautiful, blond, twenty five year old, single lady. I am fifty with a curvy figure; I often think ten pounds curvier than it should be. My hair is short and mousy brown. I am not bad looking but beside Joanne I feel frumpy."

As she arrived at the bank and headed to the teller, Vicki spotted a man working there who she had not seen on previous visits to the bank.

"Boy, is he good looking, tall and very distinguished in his grey suit. Wow! He even has a little grey at the temples; my heart did flip flops. What a hunk! I wonder who he is?"

Vicki got her money and left the bank to go shopping for a new purse to take on the plane as the ones she had were not big enough to carry her book, candies, makeup, passport and of course, money and travel documents. "There is a store I like nearby, so I will enter via the Bloor Street entrance." She wandered until she came across the bags, passing ladies shoes. Of course, she had to stop to admire a pair of red heels, then on further past the jewellery and lingerie. "I always stop here to look at all the lacy underwear; I love it and sometimes wear it even though I am single now. I still like to feel sexy."

Vicki thought: "I am not too sure whether I will wear my black slacks or my grey ones. I want to wear a sexy top so I will check my closet when I get home to see what looks best. I have quite a number of blouses and sweaters as I cannot resist buying new ones when I see something I like. There are lots of lovely bags here. I love the Michael Kors but it is lime green so I think I will take the grey suede Alexander Wang." There was a cashier at the customer sales centre so she took the bag to her. "This one will go nicely with either the black or grey slacks," thought Vicki.

"I must look good. After all, I am going to Paris and a high class fashion show."

Joanne would be with her and no matter what she was wearing she would look sexy and fantastic; she always did.

Vicki took a cab to the office and was very impressed, as usual, with the twenty storey office building that housed GFC on the twentieth floor, which was the top level, and the whole nineteenth floor. As she exited the elevator she was standing on a magnificent white marble floor. There were small green specks in the marble. She walked in a little further to a very peaceful waterfall with green velvet seats all the way around it. The walls were painted a light shade of pewter and there was a large oak desk against one wall. The receptionist raised her head from the work she was doing to say:

"Good morning Ms. Burke."

"Good morning Valerie, nice day today."

Joanne seemed very excited. Today she had her long hair up in a bun and she was wearing a navy knit dress that ended well above her knees. Vicki could see Bill, the mail boy, giving Joanne the once over; actually more than once. Vicki wished she could command some of that attention but from older men of course.

"Joanne," Vicki called over the intercom and Joanne came into the opulent office with its many artifacts and pictures. There was a complete library of every fashion magazine available and several design books as well. The furniture was all mahogany and leather with a desk and console. A large golden globe sat on the floor on a mahogany stand. There were three Chinese statues, given to Vicki when she hosted some Chinese visitors to a fashion show last year.

As Vicki sat behind the mahogany desk, Joanne sat in the comfy leather chair in front of her.

"Joanne, would you please call Mark in Travel and get our e-tickets and our itinerary for Thursday's trip. Could you also prepare the notes for tomorrow's meeting and arrange with the café downstairs to deliver coffee and scones at three o'clock?"

"Okay, I will take care of everything. I will get a few cookies as well, as they are nice with coffee and are easy to eat at a meeting."

The rest of the day was very busy and finally Vicki went home alone, again. The ache in her heart could not be filled even by the beautiful surroundings of her condominium. She needed someone to share her life with now that Joe was gone from her life and Charlie was married. "I am so alone. I need a man."

Vicki made herself some dinner and then sat and watched a few of her favourite reality shows and a game show, thinking occasionally of the man she had seen in the bank earlier that day. She finally went to bed, alone and lonely.

CHAPTER 6

TUESDAY

There was an important planning meeting at two o'clock on Tuesday. All the suits would be present and representatives from companies that GFC dealt with. Vicki was wearing her navy pin stripe "power suit" with a white silk blouse. She felt sexy in this outfit.

"I think we should add print dresses to our spring collection."

That was the suggestion from John, the manager of the fashion department and Vicki's superior. John was a good boss. He was single and everyone thought he was full of fun and easy to work with. He certainly knew his job: fabrics, styles and current trends. "I quite enjoy working with him. So, I guess, print dresses are one thing I must check out in Paris." Then Marjorie spoke up:

"I feel we should add some silk scarves to our collection as they are becoming quite popular in the fashion world for spring."

Marjorie was in her mid-fifties and had been with GFC since she arrived in Toronto from Boston twenty-one years ago. Marjorie had excellent taste in fashion so when she made a suggestion, Vicki listened and tried to comply with her wishes.

"You can never go wrong with a nice pair of shoes," John suggested. "This is every woman's dream." They discussed each suggestion in detail, especially shoes. "Wedges seem to be in this season, some with ankle straps and some are slides." said John.

The meeting ended at four o'clock and Vicki returned to her desk for an hour before heading home to pack a suitcase for Thursday's departure.

CHAPTER 7

PREPARING FOR THE TRIP

Wednesday was a slow day at the office, so Joanne and Vicki left at noon to prepare for their trip. Thursday morning Vicki had to get up early as she had a few last minute things to do before she left for her trip. They had to be at Pearson International Airport-Terminal 1 in Toronto, by five o'clock in the afternoon.

"I decided to wear the grey slacks, white sweater with a fairly low neckline that made me feel attractive, and I am wearing my black leather jacket, black pumps and, of course, carrying the new grey suede bag I bought this week," thought Vicki.

The taxi came at three-thirty in the afternoon and Vicki proceeded to the airport. They got on the 401 highway heading towards Mississauga, and wouldn't you know it, there had been an accident somewhere ahead of them and the traffic, even at that hour, was bumper to bumper. Vicki was getting very worried as she needed to be at Pearson by five o'clock. They sat in the traffic for about fifteen minutes, barely moving.

Vicki said:

"Is there an alternate route we could take?"

The driver was relatively new to Toronto and was not sure, so, he picked up his 2-way radio and called home base. He found out exactly where a large tractor-trailer, carrying a flammable substance, had over-turned. No cars were being allowed to pass due to the risk of fire. The driver was given another route on some back roads and it worked. He got Vicki to the airport by two minutes before five. She was so thankful that she doubled his tip.

Arriving at Terminal 1, Vicki met Joanne who, of course, looked great in a light blue suit, beige heels and carrying a beige purse. Her hair was tied back with curls falling down her back.

"WOW!! Is she attractive!"

They checked in and Vicki suggested they have a snack as they still had almost three hours before their flight. They found a coffee shop, which served Vicki's favourite coffee, and they sat down to a coffee and a muffin. They talked about Joanne's latest love interest, Brian.

"I am crazy about this man but he scares me a little. He is so possessive and always has to be right."

"Brian is also verbally abusive but I do not think that he would ever be physically abusive. I find him to be very exciting. I really do not like the way he talks to me but he makes up for it when we are alone at home. Brian can be very gentle and kind when he wants to be. I guess that makes him like Jekyll and Hyde."

"Joanne, please be careful. Make sure you are aware of your surroundings and what is happening at all times. I would really hate to see you get hurt in any way."

"I promise to be careful but, Vicki, he is so exciting."

They talked for another half an hour and Vicki shared her experience with Joanne.

"Joanne, you should see the gorgeous man I happened to see working in the bank the other day. I have never seen him before, but I would love to meet him. He is already on my mind and I think about him often."

Their flight left on time and was quite enjoyable. After dinner was served they managed to get a couple of hours of sleep before their arrival in Paris.

CHAPTER 8

PARIS

On their arrival in Paris, they hailed a cab to take them to their hotel in the heart of the city. The hotel was on avenue Montaigne and the legendary Champs-Elysees. It was renovated townhomes and now had beautiful suites, and a lovely, fragrant vertical garden of tropical plants, at the end of a long lobby, covered by a glass ceiling. The chasseur took Vicki and Joanne to their adjoining suites on the second floor. As she entered the very elegant surroundings, Vicki immediately spotted the two bottles of Champagne and sparkling water provided to each guest on arrival. Two small boxes of chocolates sat alongside the Champagne.

There were two queen sized beds beautifully covered in comforters of brown and cream. Four pillows were tastefully arranged on each bed, with shams to match the comforter. There were two chairs and a small, round table in the corner by the window, and a television stood at the foot of the bed. The bathroom and sink area was in a separate alcove of the room. The tub, shower and toilet were in their own separate room and two white terry robes hung on hooks by the tub.

Outside that room, was a long counter with two sinks in it and a large mirror that spanned the entire length of the counter. On a crystal dish at the side of the sink were samples of shampoo, conditioner, hand soap, lotion, a sewing kit and even a shower cap.

Friday was a free day so Vicki and Joanne browsed the local shops. They had lunch in an authentic little French bistro.

Joanne and Vicki had made reservations in the Italian Restaurant in the hotel for seven o'clock on Friday evening and arranged to meet at six in the Champagne Bar. Since it was only four thirty,

Vicki said:

"I think I will have a half hour rest before I shower and dress for dinner."

"Me too, I am a bit tired as well," agreed Joanne.

"I have my favourite little black dress for tonight with black suede shoes and a small black beaded bag," thought Vicki.

"I am feeling good."

At six o'clock, Vicki headed down to the bar. Joanne was there waiting for her. She was also wearing a little black dress. Her dress was much shorter than Vicki's. It was well above her knees and her shoes were 5" stilettos that men have nicknamed "serious fuck me shoes". She looked gorgeous.

"Let's get a table and have a drink before dinner."

As they were sipping their martinis, an older gentleman appeared at their table. He was about six feet tall, wearing a navy blazer and grey slacks. He had grey hair and looked very distinguished.

"Ladies, are you alone in Paris?"

"We are on business," Vicki told him, a little cautiously, as she was not used to men approaching her table. He must have noticed the shoes that Joanne was wearing.

"My name is Bob and I am with my son Mark. Would you care to join us for a drink?"

Joanne immediately spoke up:

"We would love to join you, Bob, thank you."

As they sat sipping their drinks, they discovered that Bob and Mark also had a seven o'clock reservation at the Italian Restaurant. Bob took out his cell phone, and after asking Vicki and Joanne to join them, made a call to change two tables for two to one table for four.

"Wow! Now we had dates for dinner. It has to be the shoes."

The restaurant was a lovely Italian balcony style setting and it reminded them of Venice. They entered the restaurant through the opulent main lobby with its beautiful French Provincial furniture. They were ushered through to the balcony. There were flowering trees in the doorway as they stepped out onto the balcony. The décor was very Italian with red and white checkered table cloths. Purple and green grapes were on trellises all around the wall. The view from the railing side was of a river which ran past the hotel. There were boats that resembled gondolas in Venice going up and down the river. As soon as they sat down, the waiter brought a carafe of wine and a menu. They all ate very well that evening.

During their dinner, Vicki caught Mark and Joanne gazing at each other on more than one occasion. As they were sitting next to each other, Mark reached over and gently placed his hand on Joanne's thigh. Joanne did not push him away. Actually she liked it, and she felt very desirable. They were laughing at each other's jokes and thoroughly enjoying each other. Noting Mark's smiling face, she gave him a wink. Both of them had a burning desire in their eyes. Mark winked back and excused the two of them from the table.

CHAPTER 9

JOANNE AND MARK

The elevator came to take them to Mark's room. When they got on the elevator, hand in hand, there were two other couples already on it. Mark eased Joanne to the back wall by placing his hand on the small of her back and gently guiding her past the other couples. With Mark's touch, Joanne felt tingles up and down her spine. Mark kissed her on the cheek. They desperately wanted to explore each other's bodies. They finally reached the eighth floor. Mark whispered:

"Okay, my sweetheart, this is our floor."

They left the elevator expectantly and hand in hand. When the elevator doors closed, Mark took Joanne in his arms and gave her what was probably the most passionate kiss she had ever had.

Desire raged through Joanne's body and she responded. She felt so weak and excited, especially when Mark's tongue began encircling her lips. This made their desire even stronger. They somehow made it to Mark's door and he used his pass card to open it, but as soon as they were inside they were in each other's arms again.

"You are so beautiful, Joanne. I cannot believe I am here with such an angel."

The kissing was exuberant and exciting and Mark unzipped Joanne's dress. As it fell to the floor, he was kissing her beautiful, firm breasts and she sighed:

"Mark, you make my blood boil in a way that no man has ever done before."

"Joanne I want you, I want to get inside your gorgeous body."

"I would love that, Mark, my dear."

There was such a desire burning inside Joanne that she couldn't wait to unzip Mark's trousers. As she did this, Mark unclipped her bra and it fell to the floor.

Joanne's excitement rose and she stepped out of her panties but left her shoes on.

"What a beautiful woman you are, Joanne."

The kissing continued and soon Mark was kissing Joanne all over, starting with her forehead, then his fingers tickled her shoulders while his tongue began to encircle each breast. He started kissing her tummy.

"I am so excited," breathed Joanne.

She started to explore Mark's body with a light touch of her fingers and then with her kisses. Mark was very fit and had a 6-pack to die for.

"I just have to kiss you all over, you are so exciting."

Her kisses were soft and gentle and made Mark more excited than ever. He took a deep breath as he wanted to slow himself down so that he could enjoy more of Joanne's attention.

When Joanne's kisses reached Mark's upper thigh he could not take it anymore and he quickly flipped her onto her back and not quite so gently entered her body. Joanne arched her back in response.

The movement quickened to a feverish pitch with lots of hot kisses and Joanne and Mark finished together.

This was a beautiful thing for both of them. They thoroughly enjoyed the wonderful experience of being together in each other's arms.

Thirty minutes later they were still together, half asleep.

"Joanne, you are fantastic."

"Mark, I have never made love like this before with a man so understanding of my needs. You are terrific."

They took a short nap before showering and dressing.

CHAPTER 10

VICKI AND BOB

After dinner Bob and Vicki went for a long walk to enjoy Paris in the evening. They strolled by a number of interesting little shops. They went through a park where there was a pond with ducks swimming.

"Bob, why don't we sit a while and enjoy the quiet of this beautiful spot?"

"Okay, it is very beautiful and peaceful."

"Back at home, with all the rush of work, we don't get time to sit and just enjoy nature and all its beauty."

"I agree, Vicki, it certainly is lovely."

They sat on a bench for about half an hour just enjoying the peacefulness of the scenery. Bob was a perfect gentleman.

On their way home, Bob found a little French café.

"Would you like to stop for a coffee?"

"That would be very nice as we have walked a long way tonight and my feet are starting to feel very heavy."

They went into the café and immediately noticed the many pastries. Apparently this café was famous for its pastries.

They just couldn't resist.

"Bob, would you like to share one of those coconut squares with me?"

"Sure, that would be great."

They sat and talked over coffee and dessert for the next hour.

Vicki found out that Bob was a widower and was showing Paris to his son before Mark's move to the United States the following week. Mark was moving to Atlanta, Georgia to accept a transfer from his company in Canada. It was a good opportunity to spend two years in Atlanta and earn triple his present salary.

They made plans to visit a museum and the Eiffel Tower on Sunday before their return home on Monday. As they walked back to the hotel, Bob took Vicki's hand and she felt warm and happy. It had been a very long time since a man paid any attention to her and she welcomed it. They reached the hotel and she told Bob: "I have to work tomorrow, but, I look forward to seeing you again on Sunday."

Bob nodded and then leaned in for a goodnight kiss. "Okay, I know it was a bit soon, but I was flattered and he was so nice." "I kissed him back."

When they parted for the night they promised to meet on Sunday for a tour of Paris.

CHAPTER 11

THE FASHION SHOW

On Saturday, Joanne and Vicki arrived early for the fashion show. They were both very anxious and excited. They were looking forward to seeing all the guests and how they were dressed for the show. Both Joanne and Vicki wondered if they were dressed suitably for the occasion, since this was Paris.

"Should we be in long gowns, or maybe suits and hats or fascinators?" After all, this was a big occasion and a first for both Joanne and Vicki.

They took their seats in the front row. It turned out that they were appropriately dressed in skirts and blouses. The show started by introducing slacks and tops. There were four models and all outfits were outstanding but Joanne and Vicki were there looking for dresses. Next, the models came out wearing coats and jackets. Then it was time for the dresses: One wrap, and one with a cowl neckline, a V-neck, three round necks and a turtle neck. Both printed and plain fabrics were used with various textures and designs. The fashions were gorgeous and they chose six prints for the spring collection. They also picked out some exquisite silk scarves.

At intermission, Joanne and Vicki had a chance to talk about the previous night. Vicki shared her plans to visit the Eiffel Tower and museum, and invited Joanne along with Mark to accompany them.

"That would be fun and I am sure Mark would enjoy it also. I know you brought your camera and I have my cell phone so maybe we can share photos."

On their return to the show, they saw a very attractive bathing suit display with bikinis, one piece suits, two piece suits and cover ups.

Then came the piece d' resistance, the bridal gowns. Joanne and Vicki really enjoyed these. Both of them were secretly hoping someday it would be them looking for a bridal gown.

"I guess this is every woman's secret dream," Vicki thought.

CHAPTER 12

SIGHTSEEING IN PARIS

Early Sunday morning, they left their rooms and went downstairs. Joanne was wearing blue jeans and a blue sweater and Vicki was wearing her black pants and a red blouse, looking hot, she hoped. They met Mark, also in jeans and a navy shirt, and Bob who wore his grey pants again but this time with a white shirt. Everyone looked good. They met in the café downstairs and began their date by enjoying a cup of coffee.

"Let's start with a tour of Chateau de Versailles. It has very well manicured gardens and one of the most famous monuments in France. I have my camera and would love to take some pictures," Vicki said.

Everyone agreed. Vicki took several shots of the four of them. Fortunately, her camera had a ten second delay so that she could get into the picture too.

"After that tour, maybe we could go for lunch and then go to the Eiffel Tower?"

They took the elevator in the Eiffel Tower. The first elevator just went up the legs of the tower. Then they transferred to another elevator that took them to the observation deck where Vicki took more pictures. The first tour was exciting and marvellous but nothing could compare with looking over the Champs-Elysees from the top of the Eiffel Tower and Vicki got some amazing pictures.

"Oh! This is absolutely fabulous. I can't imagine anything more spectacular."

They enjoyed the day with their new friends and when Bob invited them to dinner, they were pleased to accept. This time they found a delightful French Bistro. They ordered lemon sage chicken with herb roasted potatoes and rye honey cake. For dessert they had a delicious berry crumble. Bob was very attentive to Vicki and she enjoyed every minute of feeling like a lady. Joanne also enjoyed herself. Vicki could tell she really enjoyed Mark's company; this made Vicki happy to see. The friends ended the evening early, after exchanging e-mail addresses and promising to keep in touch.

CHAPTER 13

JOANNE AND BRIAN

Joanne and Vicki went to the Champagne Bar in the hotel for a night cap and to mull over the day's events. They both enjoyed their dates but knew it was a one-time thing.

Joanne, then feeling she had to talk to someone, started to tell Vicki more about the man she was currently seeing, Brian. Brian was very possessive of Joanne. Vicki guessed it was because Joanne was a knock-out and men were immediately attracted to her everywhere she went.

Joanne proceeded to tell Vicki about a prior incident that had happened between them.

One evening, Brian and Joanne were entering a cinema to see *Star Trek in 3-D*.

"Joanne, move your ass, you are holding everyone up."

"Bri, there is no one behind us."

"Just move it. I want to get some candy before the show starts."

"No need to be rude, just ask."

"Fuck you!"

Brian gave Joanne a shove. As she fell, she hit her arm on the metal door frame.

"Ouch!! That wasn't necessary Brian."

"Oh yes it was, you are too damn slow. We will never get in."

The man who was beside them in line saw what had happened and offered his help to Joanne. He picked her up from the floor and asked:

"Is there anything else I can do for you young lady?"

"Mind your own fucking business," barked Brian.

With this remark the man left and Brian and Joanne continued into the cinema.

"You are such a bloody suck. I didn't push you that hard. Learn to stand on your own two feet, why don't you?"

"Brian, I lost my balance when you shoved me and . . . ."

"Just shut up," Brian interrupted.

Joanne's whole right arm was bruised for a week. Vicki had noticed it at work at the time but when she questioned Joanne about it, she had said:

"Oh, it is really nothing. I got up during the night to pee and not wanting to turn on any lights to wake me right up, I stumbled into the bathroom missing the doorway and I hit my arm on the door frame. It hurt for a while but it is okay now and the bruising is going away."

Vicki accepted that explanation as she had no reason, at that time, to doubt her answer.

Joanne said that Brian was also verbally abusive, always demanding that she serve him and then yelling if she was not fast enough. He berated her in front of their friends and never gave her a compliment in public.

A month ago, Brian and Joanne had gone shopping for a new television for her home. They went to the local department store but nothing appealed to Joanne. Brian liked the 3-D Sony but she felt it was too expensive for her budget.

Joanne suggested:

"Why not try another store."

"Okay Joanne, but you know the best one is the one I picked out."

"It is more than I want to pay."

"Oh, just shut up and bite the bullet."

They looked at a number of sets, most of them within Joanne's price range, but Brian kept on insisting:

"You should buy the 3-D Sony."

There was also one in this store and they looked at it again but Joanne wanted the forty-two inch screen Sony Bravia. Brian was angry.

"You are so stupid, the 3-D one is the one you should buy, you ugly witch."

Joanne was very sensitive and this comment really hurt her. Joanne and Brian left the store with no purchase as Joanne was completely devastated by the treatment.

Vicki and Joanne had a long talk that evening and Vicki explained how abusive men usually get worse over time. Vicki said that when a man is insecure about himself, he tries to compensate by putting his lady down and making her feel small. If he was already hurting her, she should cut her losses and leave him NOW before he gets too dangerous and she cannot escape. Vicki hoped Joanne understood. She seemed to but she would not promise anything.

Joanne was also seeing another man, on occasion. Bill was his name. Vicki asked her about Bill and Joanne said he was a perfect gentleman at all times but not exciting and unpredictable like Brian, who Joanne said she was falling in love with. She learned to overlook his rudeness in order to enjoy the excitement she felt when she was with him.

"Always the bad boy."

CHAPTER 14

BACK TO TORONTO

Monday morning Vicki arose early, showered and dressed in blue jeans and a light blue sweater. She met Joanne in the breakfast bar of the hotel so they could have toast and coffee before calling a cab to take them to the airport for their return flight to Toronto.

Tuesday morning, back in the office, Joanne and Vicki spent most of the day filling out and processing purchase orders for their new spring line. They felt good about the choices they had made and John approved as well.

"Good work Victoria and Joanne."

They went out for a short lunch break during which time Joanne shared more stories about Brian. He was very pushy and opinionated and Vicki really wished Joanne would dump him and start dating someone else, like Bill for instance. She was so attractive and she would not have any trouble finding a new, exciting date. But, unfortunately, Joanne was hooked on this guy. Vicki knew if she said too much Joanne would rebel and spend more time with him. So all Vicki could say to her was:

"Joanne, please be careful."

CHAPTER 15

PLANNING A TRIP TO MILAN

Two months later, on Monday morning, John called Vicki into his office to inform her that she and Joanne would be leaving on the following day for another buying trip, this time to Milan, Italy. Vicki was quite excited about this one as she had always wanted to go to Milan, the fashion capital of the world. Vicki left John's office and returned to her own and immediately called Joanne in to tell her the good news.

"Joanne, I have some fabulous news. You and I are going on another buying trip, this time to Milan, Italy and we leave tomorrow evening."

"Oh Vicki, what a dream trip. I can't wait and you know Italy has some pretty handsome men."

Joanne was as excited as Vicki was and they decided they would take some time in Milan to shop for their own spring outfits.

"I am going to the bank on my way home from the office today, so I will get enough euros for both of us to save time."

Joanne thanked her and said, "See you tomorrow."

Vicki finished the purchase orders and then she had some phone calls to return. There were twenty one e-mails in her inbox so she had to take care of them before she could leave.

On her way home, Vicki stopped at the bank to purchase the euros. She walked up to the teller who she had dealt with on other occasions and placed her order. The teller excused herself:

"Sorry, I don't have enough euros on hand. I will have to get the manager to go to the vault and get some more to fill your request."

Vicki said: "Thank you" and the teller left her station. A couple of minutes later that gorgeous man Vicki had seen last time she was in the bank, appeared with her teller. He was wearing a three piece, grey, well-tailored suit with a light blue shirt and matching tie. He introduced himself as Thomas Harrison, manager of the bank, and they shook hands. Maybe it was Vicki's imagination but her whole arm tingled at his touch. Thomas invited her to take a seat in his office while he went to the vault to get the money. Her legs were like jelly, just looking at him, but she managed to walk to his office and take a seat in a very comfortable chair to wait for the manager to reappear. He came back in five minutes. That was the longest five minutes of her life. It seemed more like an hour. He had the euros she had ordered and he sat behind his desk and started to talk.

"What do you work at that requires euros so often?"

Vicki told him she was a fashion buyer, having recently been promoted from the position of design artist. She had to travel to Europe to purchase clothes for GFC's new lines.

"This week we are going to Milan."

Vicki told him:

"This happens every spring and fall. Joanne, my assistant, and I are very excited to be taking over the position of buyer. We both love to travel and this job suits us very well."

"What a great job," Thomas said.

"Travelling to Europe must be quite a perk."

Thomas inquired if Vicki was married and she told him "divorced". He told her he was a widower. His wife had passed away five years ago from breast cancer. Vicki offered her sincere condolences and he smiled his acceptance. He then asked:

"Would you consider having dinner with me on your return from Milan?"

"How can I control my excitement? This is a dream come true. My gorgeous banker just asked me out."

"Where will he take me?"

"What is he like?"

"Will he like me?"

"What will I wear?"

"What will I say?"

"I don't want to say too much on a first date and scare him off."

Vicki managed to control her feelings and answered very politely.

"I would love to join you for dinner." *"Actually I would be willing to join him for a lot more than just dinner, but I kept my cool."*

"When are you returning to your office?"

Vicki told him she would be back in the office on Monday morning and he agreed to give her a call.

CHAPTER 16

VICKI AND BARB

Vicki could hardly wait to get home and tell her story to her neighbour and good friend Barb Jones. Barb had been Vicki's neighbour since she moved into the condo. She was very considerate and had offered her help with Vicki's move. Barb was forty five years old and had never been married. She was engaged when she was twenty two but her boyfriend was killed in a plane crash. Barb just had not met another man she wanted to get close to. Barb and Vicki had become good friends looking out for each other since they both lived alone.

"You are travelling a lot these days. I guess this is your busy season," Barb commented.

"Very busy, but a lot of fun, I really love my job. However, I have something even more exciting to share with you."

"What! Tell me."

"Okay, today I met a dreamy man; he is the manager of the bank that I use. He asked me to dinner when I return from Milan. Oh, Barb you should see him, tall, dark hair with grey at the temples, slim and a fantastic dresser. I could seriously fall for this guy."

"I wish you the best, he sounds wonderful. I would love to meet someone too."

Barb made tea for Vicki and they talked for another hour mainly about the pros and cons of internet dating. This seemed like one of the best ways to meet people these days. Social media was definitely the way of the future. Then Vicki went home to dream about Thomas, "my banker."

CHAPTER 17

THOMAS HARRISON

Thomas had worked as a banker since he graduated from the University of Toronto at the age of twenty four. He started off as a teller and then was promoted to Chief Accountant. Nine years ago, Thomas was given a branch to manage in Scarborough. It was a small branch with only fifteen employees. Thomas was well liked and did an excellent job for eight years. Then a promotion was offered to him, a much larger branch in downtown Toronto. He was a bit nervous about the size of this branch but his superior assured him that he had the skills to handle the job.

Thomas accepted the challenge and had been in his new branch for almost a year now.

On Monday afternoon this very charming woman of fifty-something, entered the bank to purchase euros for a trip to Milan. Thomas felt so lucky that she chose the branch that he managed. Since his beloved wife passed away five years ago he had not dated or even seen anyone he could be interested in, until today, that is. Her name was Victoria Burke and she was a divorcee. Thomas found himself thinking about her the whole time she was away. The excitement of calling her on her return for a date was getting the better of him. He was sitting in his office planning how to ask her. He felt like a young university student again with raging hormones.

CHAPTER 18

MILAN, ITALY

Tuesday evening came quickly and Joanne and Vicki were off again, this time to Milan. Vicki wore a black and white dress; it was very striking. She wanted to look good on arrival in Milan. Joanne wore a dress as well; it was blue and very short but, of course, she could carry this look off. They had a reservation at the best hotel in Milan. It was in the heart of the fashion district just facing the entrance to the Galleria Vittorio Emanuel. Their accommodations were out of this world. Vicki's room had a green silk duvet on a king size bed too beautiful to even sit on so Vicki chose an armchair in the corner. In front of the window was a small table with a vase of freshly cut flowers in the centre. On the dresser there was a basket of fresh fruit and in the minibar water and soft drinks. There were also some small bottles of wine and liquor. On the dresser, beside the coffee pot, were some snacks; potato chips, peanuts and candy bars. Since they were both tired and it was now Wednesday morning, they decided to go downstairs to La Cupola Lounge for breakfast and then they went to their rooms for a couple of hours to rest from the trip. That afternoon they went sightseeing and also did some window shopping.

On Thursday, they met three suppliers and examined many differently styled suits. The fabrics were exquisite. Then, on Friday, they looked mainly at dresses but did find time to check out the shoes and of course, Vicki wanted them all. Then they had to decide which suppliers with whom to make out purchase orders. It was a very busy two days. When Saturday finally came around they decided to go to some upscale stores. After all, they were now buying for themselves and in Milan, no less.

Vicki and Joanne set out for Quadrilatero d'oro, the most elite shopping area in Milan. They tried on many dresses in several shops. In one of the boutiques Vicki spotted a green dress.

"Joanne, what do you think of this?"

"Oh Vicki, try it on."

Vicki thought this would be perfect for her date with Thomas when she returned to Toronto. The dress was form-fitting with a V-neckline. It fell to just below the knee, and it was made of silk and had sparkles around the neckline.

"I feel like a goddess in this dress."

"Joanne, what do you think?"

Vicki could tell by the look on her face, even before Joanne spoke, that she looked stunning. Vicki added a pair of strappy beige heels and a small beige silk clutch.

"**WOW**" "Thomas, look out!!"

Vicki and Joanne flew out of Rome but not until they had a tour of the Vatican. Vicki had always wanted to see Vatican City.

Vatican City is the world's smallest city. Vicki and Joanne entered via St. Peter's Square where there was an unbelievable eighty three foot Egyptian obelisk in the centre. They carried on to St. Peter's Basilica where they saw the famous Swiss guards. They took the elevator and then there were over 300 steps, to get to the top and look over the City. Vicki had to wait at the bottom of these steps, as she had trouble climbing. She also found it almost impossible to walk down steps but did not know why.

"Boy, is this ever beautiful!" said Joanne.

Then they visited the Vatican Museum and then the Sistine Chapel with its magnificent paintings on the ceiling and on the walls. Both of them admitted that they had never seen anything like this before. They were so happy that they had added this tour to their trip.

Vicki and Joanne went home on Sunday night and crashed until Monday morning. Vicki did not even unpack her suitcase before her head hit the pillow. It was quite an intense trip and she was feeling very tired.

CHAPTER 19

WAITING TO HEAR FROM THOMAS

Monday morning Vicki dragged herself out of bed, got a shower, washed her hair and dressed for work. She chose a brown dress with a shawl collar. Vicki liked this dress as it was a knit and very comfortable and since she was still tired from her trip, she did not feel like being fussy. For some unknown reason, Vicki's feet were feeling like lead and she had trouble picking them up. She was shuffling a little as she tried to walk. Vicki knew she was tired and attributed her symptoms to this fact and just carried on. She figured she would be feeling better tomorrow, after a good night's sleep. Even though she was tired, Vicki's mind was elsewhere; on Thomas. She stared at the phone most of the morning waiting for him to call.

"What if he doesn't call? I think I will go crazy. Maybe he was just being polite when he said he would take me to dinner."

Joanne and Vicki had lunch sent in and ate in the lunchroom. Vicki couldn't miss his call.

During lunch, Joanne seemed a little sluggish, and she was not eating.

"Are you okay, Joanne?" Vicki asked.

Before Joanne could answer, she tried to stand up but, as she got up, Vicki knew from the look on her face that she was not well. As she leaned forward to stand, she passed out. Vicki rushed to her side as she regained consciousness. It was just a momentary syncopal attack but not a common occurrence for Joanne, so Vicki made her promise to see her doctor.

All afternoon Vicki sat wondering what she would do if Thomas did not call. She started to pace around the office. "What a basket case you are becoming." At four thirty, just as she was packing up to go home, her phone rang. Vicki practically jumped out of her skin.

"I hope it's him, I hope it's him."

Vicki was so afraid to answer the phone in case it was not Thomas. She took a deep breath and picked it up. "Hello, Victoria speaking."

Then she heard the most wonderful sound in the world:

"Hello Victoria, this is Thomas. Do you remember me from the bank?"

"Did I remember him? I have been thinking of nothing else."

"Yes Thomas I do remember you, how are you?" Vicki breathed a sigh of relief.

"I am just fine, how was your trip to Milan?"

"It was very successful; we ordered lots of lovely things for our spring/summer collection."

"I didn't want to call too soon, I wanted to give you time to get settled but I did promise to take you out for dinner. What night is good for you?"

"Well, Thomas, I am free on Thursday evening if that suits you?"

"Yes wonderful, I will make a reservation and pick you up at seven o'clock."

"Thank you Thomas, I will be looking forward to it."

"If he only knew how much I was looking forward to it and the possibility of even more."

"Please call me Tom."

"And you may call me Vicki."

"Good night, Vicki."

"Good night, Tom."

After that call Vicki floated home, dreaming of her date on Thursday.

"How am I going to survive until then?"

When Thomas had called her Monday afternoon he had asked very sheepishly if she remembered him and he held his breath waiting for her answer. They had planned their first date for Thursday evening. Thomas felt he had to make this date very special. He thought the Rainbow Suite which was a new, high class restaurant, would impress a lady. Just thinking about their date made him feel sensations that he had not felt in a long, long time, but at least he knew those feelings were still there.

CHAPTER 20

JOANNE'S NEWS

On Tuesday after work, Joanne visited her doctor. She was feeling fine by this time and almost cancelled the appointment. The doctor did blood tests, probably knowing the diagnosis, but just for confirmation he ordered a Beta HCG and urinalysis.

"Congratulations Joanne, you are pregnant."

Joanne was flabbergasted and she started to cry.

"No need to cry, what is the problem? I thought you would be happy."

"No doctor, I am single and I don't know who the father is."

"I'm very sorry, but you do have options and when you decide what you are going to do I am here to help you."

"Now I have a dilemma. Who is the father?"

Brian—"I hope not, he would not make a good father or husband."

Bill—This would not be too bad, he is very nice."

Mark—"God Forbid!"

CHAPTER 21

FIRST DATE—VICKI AND TOM

As Vicki showered after work on Thursday, she was thinking of her first date and the beautiful green dress she was going to wear.

"Hope to cause you some palpitations on first sight, Tom, LOOK OUT!!!"

Tom arrived right at seven o'clock and he looked fantastic and very debonair in his navy three piece suit.

"I have a thing for a man in a suit."

"Oh yes!"

When Tom first laid eyes on Vicki he smiled politely but the blush on his cheeks gave away his true feelings and Vicki felt so good knowing that he liked what he saw.

"Vicki, you look so beautiful."

"Thank you and you look very handsome."

If he could read her mind Vicki would be in big trouble. She was picturing him without that gorgeous suit, his rippling muscles bare and a nice tight butt that she would love to get her hands on. But she kept this thought to herself.

"I made reservations at the Rainbow Suite, a new restaurant with good reviews. Hope this is okay?"

"Of course, that is wonderful."

"I would have gone anywhere with him that night."

When they arrived at the restaurant, the maître d' seated them by the beautiful bay window. All the natural oak wood made the surroundings very elegant. The tables were covered with crisp white linen tablecloths. A large grandfather clock with dazzling gold chimes stood regally in the corner. There was a fire burning in the gas fireplace which was in the middle of the room. Fresh flowers in crystal vases adorned every table. Tom ordered a bottle of Grattamacco, a Tuscan red wine at $85.00 a bottle. Vicki just knew he would have excellent taste in wine.

"What would you like to have for dinner, Vicki?"

"Why don't you order for both of us? I like anything except sea food."

Tom raised his glass and said:

"Cheers and here is to a lovely evening with a very lovely lady."

Vicki raised her glass as well:

"Cheers Tom."

When the waiter approached their table, Tom ordered:

Two starter salads

Two fillet mignon steaks

Vegetables and baked potatoes

While they were waiting for their dinners to arrive, they were sipping wine and Tom reached across the table and took Vicki's hand.

"It is so nice to have a beautiful woman across the table from me. I am flattered that you accepted my invitation."

"Tom, you are a very handsome man and I was honoured to be invited."

Their dinners arrived and they both enjoyed the food.

"Would you care for a dessert, Vicki?"

"No thank you, Tom, but I would like a coffee."

Tom ordered two cups of coffee and they sat for another half hour.

What a start to a first date! Vicki couldn't have dreamed of such a wonderful man and a perfect start to what was quickly shaping up to be the perfect date.

Their evening ended on a good note as well. Tom walked Vicki to her door and they shared several minutes of hugging and kissing.

"I have two tickets to the Princess of Wales Theatre for Saturday night; would you care to join me?"

"Thank you, I would love to."

Vicki was so happy that he wanted her to join him again that it didn't even cross her mind to ask what was playing. Frankly, she would have gone anywhere he suggested just as long as they were together. Vicki did not invite him in as she didn't want to appear anxious or easy. It was all she could do to enter her suite alone. She would have loved to have Tom in her arms all night long. At least now she could dream about Saturday night.

"What will I wear?"

"I have a lot of nice outfits."

"I think a dress. No maybe a suit."

"I want to look especially good so hopefully there will be a third date."

Saturday finally came and Vicki chose a black suit with a white silk blouse, quite smart looking, she thought. The show was Les Miserables which Vicki had seen a few months ago in the movie theatre. It seemed completely different on the live stage. She thought that possibly she enjoyed it more on stage or maybe it was because she was with Tom and they were holding hands.

After the show they went to a small café for coffee. It was a popular café and was quite busy following the show, so they took their coffee outside to the patio. Tom put his jacket over Vicki's shoulders as it was a bit chilly that evening. They talked about their families, jobs and generally their lives. Tom seemed quite lonely since his wife died; he had two children, a son Alex and a daughter Melissa. Alex and his wife Bonnie had been married for six years but had no children. His daughter Melissa was married to Brian and they had two boys, Justin and Raymond. However, they were all very busy with their own lives and taking the boys to hockey games, Karate and many other activities consumed much of their time. Tom, therefore, did not see his children as often as he would have liked.

CHAPTER 22

JOANNE

When Monday morning came Joanne knew she had to tell Vicki that she was pregnant. Vicki was surprised at Joanne's news.

"Who is the lucky father?"

"I am not sure," she sobbed.

"I have three possibilities. I hope it isn't Brian, I know he would freak out."

"Brian and Bill always used a condom but when I had sex with Mark in Paris, we did not use protection. I think it must be Mark's baby but when I am eight months pregnant I will have DNA testing done to confirm the father."

"What are you going to do now?"

Joanne discussed her options.

Option 1—Adoption. This didn't seem too possible as Joanne really loved babies and knew she had to keep the child.

Option 2—Tell Mark. Should she tell Mark? He had just started a new job and Joanne didn't want to cause him any trouble.

Option 3—Raise the child herself. She could keep her secret and raise the baby on her own.

This would take some finessing. She would have to tell Brian who didn't know about Bill or Mark. Joanne was very frightened by this prospect but in a few short months it would be evident and then trickier to explain. When Joanne told Brian that she was pregnant, he absolutely lost it.

"I thought we were careful, we always used a condom. I don't want a kid so what the hell are you going to do about it?"

"First of all Brian, you are not the father."

"What! You little whore." "You mean you have been sleeping around with someone else?"

He picked a glass up from the table and hurled it towards Joanne. She ducked and it just missed her left shoulder. Joanne was terrified. Now she had a baby to protect.

"Who is the fucking father? Who have you been screwing around with? Nobody is as good for you as me and you know it. How could you do that to me, you little slut?"

Joanne knew he was far too upset to talk rationally so she left but promised to talk the next day.

"I am not feeling well so I will talk to you tomorrow and answer your questions."

When the next day came, Joanne phoned Brian as she was afraid to talk in person. She did not admit who the father was. She just said:

"You don't know him."

Brian exploded!!

"You are a giant slut, Joanne, and I don't want anything to fucking do with you ever."

Joanne was crushed but not surprised as Brian never could accept situations he could not control.

That night Joanne was at home alone. It was about ten thirty and there was a loud knock on her door.

"At ten thirty at night I am not going to answer the door. It can't be good."

Joanne ignored the knocking and it finally stopped. As she peeked through the curtains, she could see Brian storming off towards his car which was parked on the street in front of her house. He sat for a minute or two and then drove off squealing the tires as he went.

The next morning at work, Joanne related the incident to Vicki.

"I am afraid of what he might do."

"If I were you, I would tell the police and ask them to keep an eye out for his car at your house."

"Well, it was only one incident and maybe I am imagining the danger. I think I will wait and see."

"Okay, but just be careful Joanne, you have to take care of yourself now that you have a new life depending on you."

"I promise to be careful."

Joanne walked home from work that day as she wanted the exercise and she lived just forty minutes away. As she was walking, she had the feeling that someone was following her, but, when she turned around to check, there was nobody there. She continued with her walk thinking to herself that she was just imagining things.

When Joanne was about ten minutes from her home she heard the familiar sound of Brian's car. She knew it because he had a special muffler that was louder than most.

Joanne didn't turn to look; she just ducked into a variety store that was nearby. Joanne's friend worked in the store and when she told her what was happening the friend said:

"I am not alone in the store today; I have help so I will excuse myself for a few minutes and walk you home."

"Thank you so much, Marie. You are a good friend."

With Joanne safely at home and her doors and windows locked, Brian drove off.

For the next week Joanne took a taxi home from work every day. She did go to the police but they said:

"Since Brian has not committed a crime, there is really nothing we can do at this time. Just try to stay away from him."

Joanne had never seen Brian in the early morning, as he liked to sleep in, so she felt safe walking to work as she had always done. It was a nice, bright, sunny morning and Joanne was taking her time enjoying the lovely weather, walking and doing a little window shopping on the way. Suddenly a car pulled up to the curb and a man jumped out. It was Brian and he was irate. He grabbed Joanne and forced her into his car.

"What are you doing? Where are you taking me?"

"Just shut your trap and sit still. I am taking you for the ride of your life," he said as he sped off down the street.

"When we get there, I am going to rearrange your face so no man will ever want you again. That is what you deserve after what you did to me."

"Brian PLEASE!"

"Shut up, we are almost there."

In a few minutes they arrived at the Rouge Beach in Scarborough. It was very quiet as it was the middle of the week.

"Get out of the car NOW!"

"Okay, okay I'm coming."

"Just do what I say."

Brian took a small folding knife from his pocket and Joanne took a deep, frightened breath.

"I am going to cut your face so much that you will be scarred for life. But first I want details of your fucking around."

"No Brian. I'm sorry I hurt you," Joanne sobbed.

"Not as sorry as you are going to be, you stupid bitch."

"What can I do?"

"Tell me the truth."

"I have told you the truth Brian. There was you and then Bill, on occasion, but neither of you is the baby's father."

"Then tell me who is."

"It happened in Paris and it was someone you don't know."

"You mean it was a bloody Frenchman. That's the limit. I am much better than that."

"He wasn't French, he was a Canadian visiting Paris."

Brian started to get extremely more upset with every word Joanne spoke.

"Whoever it was, he is not as good as me," he said angrily, "and you know it."

Then Brian grabbed Joanne's arm and pushed her to the ground. He opened the pocket knife and started towards her.

"Let's try it on your arm first just to make sure it is sharp enough."

He took a swipe at Joanne's left arm just below the elbow. She cried out and Brian laughed. Then he directed his attention to her face. Joanne's arm was bleeding and she was in pain but nevertheless she put her hands up to protect her face as Brian moved closer with the knife.

"Drop the knife and step away."

Thank God! The police had arrived. Vicki had called them when Joanne failed to show up at work and they traced her position from the GPS on her cell phone, which was in her purse.

The police took Brian away in handcuffs as Vicki drove Joanne to the hospital to have her arm stitched and have her and the baby checked out.

CHAPTER 23

TOM AND VICKI

Tom and Vicki didn't see each other for the next couple of weeks and she was getting a bit worried. "Maybe he doesn't like me as much as I think."

Vicki was buried under purchase orders when the phone rang and it startled her.

"There is a call for you Vicki, from Tom, shall I put it through?"

"Yes, thank you Joanne."

"Hello, Victoria here."

"This is Tom. Vicki, sorry it has taken me so long to call again but I have been very busy at work, as my accountant has been off. She had to have an appendectomy and I have been covering her work. I couldn't get a replacement on short notice. I just called to tell you there is a cocktail party on Friday evening at the Delta Chelsea Hotel for all bankers and their guests. Would you consider accompanying me?"

"I would love to, thank you."

"I will get back to you with the details and thank you. It is always better when you have someone to share your time with."

For the rest of the afternoon Vicki's mind was not on her work.

"He called me back, I am so excited." "I thought we got along very well but I didn't know how Tom was feeling. Now I feel better and the dreaming continues."

CHAPTER 24

BARBARA

As she awakened to the sound of the birds singing on a beautiful morning, Barb opened her eyes and looked at her clock.

"Four thirty in the morning."

"I love your singing but why so early and why is there a tree so close to my bedroom window?"

Barb tried to go back to sleep but to no avail.

At five thirty: "Guess I might as well start my day."

After brushing her teeth and washing her face, Barb headed out to her computer. **No New Messages** flashed on the screen.

"I feel very alone now that Vicki has Tom."

With that thought in mind, Barb started peeking at a dating site. Lots of thoughts were running through her mind.

"Maybe I could find my *special someone* on line, as I don't frequent bars or dance halls. I need somewhere to meet men."

The site asked for her area of residence and she typed in Toronto. Then the age of the man she was looking for so Barb gave a range of 40-55. Some pictures came up as samples of what the site offered. She liked what she saw so decided to go a little further. She was asked to provide her Visa number to join for a trial period of six months. The price seemed reasonable so she hit the OK button and became a member. Barb had to put her profile on the site with a picture, which she found on her computer.

"Now, I guess, I wait to see if anyone likes my profile. I don't feel comfortable approaching the men, so I will just wait. Old fashioned, I guess."

As it was Saturday, Barb only had to work at the flower shop until noon. She was so excited to go home to check her computer wondering if she appealed to anyone.

Maybe none.

Maybe several.

What fun!

CHAPTER 25

INTERNET DATING

When she arrived home, there were three messages on the computer from three different men. Barb eagerly sat down to read their information. She was so excited she could barely read the screen. The first man was only thirty years old:

"I guess he is looking for an older woman, but I am not a cougar," so she hit *delete*.

The second was a business man in his mid-forties. His picture looked very nice; he was slim and well dressed with expertly styled hair. His name was Bill. The third man was scruffy looking and would not suit Barb's refined taste. She decided to answer Bill. They planned to meet on Sunday, which was the next day, at a coffee shop just down the street. She didn't tell him where she lived just to ensure her safety. They met, at the coffee shop, at four in the afternoon. As Barb walked in she was looking for the blue and white sweater he said he would be wearing. She spotted him right away sitting at a table in the corner. He looked very respectable, clean and well groomed and she already knew he spoke well as they had made their plans over the telephone. Barb's heart skipped a beat.

"Could it really be this easy?"

She approached the table and Bill stood up to greet her.

"A gentleman, no less."

He extended his hand and then pulled the chair out for her to sit.

They sat down and then she knew. He opened his mouth to ask her what she would like. Barb saw black and broken teeth, possibly from many years of smoking. Even from across the table she could detect his bad breath.

"Oh, I am not going to ever kiss that!"

"Why would a person who obviously cares about his looks and dresses with a refined demeanor not look after his mouth?" She could not comprehend such a lack of concern.

They finished their coffee and a very pleasant conversation, but Bill was not for her. She returned home feeling very disappointed.

Monday came and Barb went to work making floral arrangements for people in love and how she longed to be one of them. She couldn't wait to get home to her computer and hopefully her new life. There was one e-mail from a man named Joe but he was *temporarily unemployed* "DELETE."

For the next few days there were no messages but on Friday when Barb approached her computer a message was flashing. Michael had sent an e-mail. Michael was forty nine years old, a widower, his wife having died four years previously. His picture was respectable; he was an accountant and looking to meet a nice lady. Barb responded and they set up a date at a large restaurant, for six p.m. Saturday. She wanted lots of people around as she didn't know this man.

Barb arrived precisely at six and Michael met her at the door. He was nicely dressed and groomed and had a lovely smile. Again her hopes soared.

"Maybe this is my Prince Charming?"

"He certainly has a lovely smile. I really hope Michael is the one."

They sat at a table by the window and ordered steaks and salads, and a bottle of Pinot Grigio and they began a nice conversation. No sooner had they started talking when his cell phone rang. He excused himself and took the call. Arriving back at the table he poured two glasses of wine and then received a text message which he promptly answered. Barb was wondering why he didn't leave his phone at home. During dinner he received and answered three more messages.

"I am afraid I can't compete with a mobile device."

"Michael was certainly not for me."

Another disappointment.

Barb was feeling down all day Sunday. She kept checking her computer but no messages appeared. By Wednesday there was an e-mail from George. They spoke on the phone and everything was *me me me.* He was so conceited and it made Barb feel like she was nothing. So, no date with George.

Thursday morning Barb was filling an order for red and pink roses with a little baby's breath and she was almost crying for the lucky lady who was to receive these beautiful flowers. She managed to take down the name and address to send them out. She asked this extremely attractive gentleman who was sending them if he would like to include a card. He said:

"Yes, just put Happy Birthday Mom and sign it Giovanni."

Barb was impressed by this gesture of love for his mother and she told him so.

"Giovanni, what a kind thing to do for your mother on her birthday. She is truly blessed."

"You must have a special someone in your life who sends you flowers, a beautiful woman like you."

She could hardly answer as her throat was choking up.

"No, not at the moment, I'm afraid."

Barb went home that night praying for a message on her computer. As fate would have it, there was one e-mail.

"I only need one."

It was from Kevin. He was 53 years old, quite good looking and he was a lawyer.

"This sounds promising."

They set up a meeting Friday evening again at the coffee shop. Barb was there first and when Kevin arrived she was shocked to see him wearing jeans and a sleeveless undershirt sometimes called a "wife beater shirt". Not even a T-shirt but an undershirt. He had a tattoo of a snake on his left arm. Barb could also detect the odour of beer on his breath. They talked for a long time and she learned that this man had plenty of money; he had a large home in Rosedale, a cottage on Lake Muskoka and a small plane which he piloted.

Everything seemed perfect but the sleeveless shirt and alcohol on his breath bothered her. And this was for a first meeting. What would he be like around the house (yuk).

"Kevin was not for me."

When Barb got home, again feeling very rejected, her phone rang and when she answered it, she was surprised to hear Giovanni who had ordered roses from the flower shop yesterday. Barb always attached her card with her phone number at the flower shop, and her private cell number, to her invoices in case of delivery problems.

"Do you remember me?" said Giovanni.

Of course she did. He was a middle aged, ruggedly handsome, Italian gentleman. Barb said:

"Of course, was there something wrong with your order?"

"Oh no" he said:

"I called to ask you if you would like to join me for dinner some time."

Barb was thrilled and readily accepted. Giovanni picked her up at seven o'clock on Saturday. They were going to 7 West Café. When they arrived, the lights were low which made the restaurant seem very romantic. There were candles on the tables to add to the ambiance and Barb was there with a good looking, Italian gentleman. What could be better? They took their seats at a quiet table in the corner. They ordered red wine and penne pasta in brandy sauce. The dinner was absolutely delicious and came with bread that they dipped into a mixture of olive oil, balsamic vinegar and oregano.

"Please call me John. That is the English form of Giovanni."

"And my nickname is Barb for Barbara."

The dinner was wonderful and they talked for over three hours.

John invited Barb to go to a soccer game with him the following weekend and she eagerly accepted.

They have been dating regularly ever since.

CHAPTER 26

BOB

Friday came and as Vicki was dreaming about another wonderful evening with Tom, she received an e-mail from Bob, the man she met in Paris.

> Hi Vicki:
> I have been thinking about you a lot since Paris. I will be in Toronto next week and would love to take you out for dinner. I am staying at the Four Seasons Hotel and, if you agree, I will make a reservation at their Café Boulud for Wednesday at seven o'clock? Anticipating your reply.
> Your Friend,
> Bob

Vicki was very surprised to hear from Bob. She was very flattered by his invitation.

> Hi Bob:
> Thank you for your e-mail. What a pleasant surprise. I would love to join you for dinner on Wednesday but I must tell you that I am currently seeing someone here in Toronto. If you still want to take me to dinner, please let me know the details and I would be happy to join you.
> Thanks again,
> Vicki

Bob replied to her e-mail saying:

> I am sorry you are seeing someone now but I
> would still like to take you to dinner, just in
> case there is a chance for us to be more than just
> friends.

Vicki agreed to go as a friend and Bob arranged to pick her up at six o'clock the following Wednesday.

CHAPTER 27

VICKI AND TOM

Later that day, following a busy day at work, Vicki showered and dressed for the cocktail party with Tom.

"I think I will dazzle Tom with a short black cocktail dress, silver flats, and a small black beaded bag." Vicki really did not like wearing flat shoes but lately her feet felt so heavy. She was much more comfortable in flats, so she chose a pair of very pretty silver shoes for the occasion.

Vicki decided to tell Tom about her arrangement with Bob on the following Wednesday as she did not want there to be any secrets between them. Tom deserved to know what she was doing. Vicki could tell he was a little jealous but he wished her a good time.

Vicki met a number of Tom's banking friends and had a good evening, but after the cocktail party the fun really began. Tom invited her to his home for coffee. She was delighted and, of course, accepted.

They drove to an older area in Toronto between Mt. Pleasant and Yonge Street. Tom had a beautiful, large, bungalow. As they arrived, the automatic lights in the shared driveway came on and they drove carefully down the narrow drive between the two houses to the garage in the back of Tom's property. They parked the car and walked down a narrow path at the side of the driveway. There were a few flowers and several lights to lead the way to the front of the house and the front door. There were panel windows on either side of the door adorned with stained glass.

Vicki was very pleasantly surprised at the lovely décor inside the house. The large foyer was painted in a light cream colour with a bench made of oak that had a drawer to store gloves, scarves, hats, and other small items. An ornate Chinese vase with a number of ceramic flowers on the front sat on a long, oak table and the vase was filled with tall, fresh irises. They looked beautiful. All of this was at the front door to greet Tom's guests. His home was very tastefully decorated. His late wife must have had excellent taste and Vicki knew he missed her. They proceeded through to the back of the house, down a hallway where some of Tom's art collection was displayed, and into the kitchen. It was painted a light green, had dark coloured marble counter tops and a white ceramic floor. Attached to the kitchen was a small sunroom with a table and two chairs, perfect for breakfast. Tom put on the coffee.

"Would you like to sit in the front room by the fire?" asked Tom.

"Yes, will you join me while you are waiting for the coffee?" said Vicki.

They proceeded through the dining room with its mahogany dining suite and buffet containing many very beautiful figurines, plates, cups, a crystal wine decanter and other treasures gathered over the years. The front room was also very tastefully decorated and boasted two velvet chairs, one on either side of the fireplace. There were several pieces of art on the walls, mainly photos and paintings from places Tom and his wife had visited over the years. Vicki was particularly fond of the one from Costa Rica which depicted a beach scene with white-face monkeys, called capuchin, in the trees in the foreground of the picture. There was a beautiful pair of silver peacocks on the mantle over the fireplace. A small, glass table in one corner of the room held a lovely Chinese lamp. It was beige in colour with a blue and rust floral design. On another wall was a credenza with books on top which were held upright by two silver elephants. Tom started the gas fireplace and they sat on either side of the fire waiting for the coffee. They talked about their jobs and family. Vicki learned, not unexpectedly, that Tom loved his family and that they returned the feeling. When Tom excused himself to get the coffee, she strategically moved to the couch hoping that Tom would sit beside her. It worked. He pulled up a small table for the coffee and cookies he had also put out and he sat right beside her.

"Good, my strategy is working; I want to be close enough to feel the warmth from his body."

Vicki took his hand as he sat beside her. His skin felt soft and warm. They sat for a couple of hours, holding hands and listening to classical music which they both loved. It was getting late so Vicki said:

"I must leave soon."

"Tom, you can just call me a cab. I don't want you to have to drive me home, I know you are tired."

Tom leaned over and kissed her and thanked her for the consideration.

"I have a better idea. Why don't you stay here with me tonight and I will drive you home in the morning?"

Vicki was so excited nothing could have made her happier. This was her dream coming true. Her emotions were running wild, just like that of a much younger woman.

"But I guess: I am not dead yet."

Vicki had thoughts of kissing him and holding him close to her body.

"Thank you, Tom, I would love to stay."

They then kissed again and she was in heaven.

They cleared the dishes and then went to Tom's master suite. The bedroom was very lovely in brown with large, oversized cream coloured pillows on the bed. Knowing that Tom had not had anyone in that big king sized bed since his wife passed away, Vicki made a suggestion that they use the guest room. She felt that this would be a little bit more comfortable for Tom. It had a queen sized bed. This room was just down the hall from the master suite and the washroom was in the hall but right next to the guest room. The room was delicately decorated with a blue floral bedspread and two white, fluffy, scatter rugs on top of the dark hardwood floor.

There were two small lamps with glass floral shades on the night tables at either side of the bed. Tom seemed relieved at her suggestion. They were both tired but could not stay away from each other any longer. They stepped into the bedroom together, kissing and hugging each other. Tom ran his fingers through her hair and kissed her forehead.

"You are so lovely," Tom whispered as he turned his hand over and gently stroked her cheek with the back of his fingers. Then he gently kissed her mouth.

"Vicki, you feel so soft, like a kitten, my kitten."

As they kissed, Vicki's fingers were in Tom's beautiful hair, so soft and when she kissed his head she could smell the scent of musk. They held each other so tightly Vicki could barely breathe. Tom reached for the zipper on her dress. He slowly unzipped it.

"What lovely white skin you have Vicki. I'm going to kiss it from top to bottom."

This he did until her dress fell to the floor in a soft pool. She kicked off her silver shoes and soon after her bra and panties. She was so happy that she had decided to wear her new, black lace bra and matching lace panties. Vicki was so excited she could hardly contain her feelings.

"This beautiful man and I were making love."

Vicki helped Tom out of his shirt and trousers. Now he was just in his boxers.

"Tom, you look so sexy."

Tom had chosen tight, black boxers that turned Vicki on. What a handsome man. How could she be so lucky?

They continued kissing as Tom eased her towards the bed. When he joined her, the boxers were with her dress on the floor. The kissing got stronger and stronger. Vicki was so thrilled to finally be able to plant kisses on this gorgeous man. His body smelled of delicious cologne that she did not recognise, but she loved the manly scent.

Vicki kissed his forehead, neck and shoulders one at a time, very slowly and deliberately. Then she kissed his muscular chest from one side to the other encircling his nipples with her tongue. She could tell she was getting to Tom as he started squirming around a little but she continued. She kissed his stomach with its tight muscles. Then, as she was moving even lower, Tom took her face in his hands and softly kissed it all over. It felt so good. Vicki thought she would lose the little bit of control she had left. He kissed her chest paying special attention to each breast. Again she nearly surrendered completely.

Tom was now massaging Vicki's breasts tenderly and softly.

"Vicki, my kitten, you are lovely."

Soon Tom was on top of her and he very gently entered her beautiful body. Vicki moaned.

"Are you okay, dear, should I stop?"

"I am fine, Honey, and please don't stop."

They were in heaven being as one, body and soul. They fell asleep in each other's arms.

"I can't wait to sleep with him again, as he is even better than I could have imagined. I didn't think anyone so fabulous existed or that I could find such joy."

Vicki's wish came true as Tom invited her to stay the weekend with him. They went shopping on Saturday afternoon as she only had the dress she was wearing. Tom let her borrow a sweat suit and sandals that his daughter Melissa had left on her last trip. They visited a few stores and she purchased a pair of jeans, sneakers, two sweaters, black lace underwear, of course, and a long white, silk nightie. Then they went to the drug store so Vicki could buy a toothbrush, hairspray and a few other personal items.

That evening they went to a movie after having dinner at Tom's home.

"And, guess what? Tom is a great cook, I really lucked out."

The movie was *It's Complicated* with Meryl Streep, Alec Baldwin and Steve Martin. They both enjoyed the comedy and had a good laugh.

Saturday night they made love again and Vicki felt she just couldn't get enough of this man. Sunday morning came far too soon and she had to go home to prepare for work on Monday. Tom drove her home and she invited him in. He stayed for coffee and a tuna sandwich as it was lunch time and they were both feeling hungry.

Vicki felt she had never had such a wonderful weekend and couldn't wait to tell Barb. Barb was thrilled at her news and said she was so jealous. She had been dating Giovanni for a while now but they had not stayed together yet.

CHAPTER 28

VICKI AND BOB

On Wednesday, Vicki was still dreaming about her weekend with Tom but she had promised Bob she would go to dinner with him. Vicki usually danced around the house when she was getting ready to go out but this time her feet refused to cooperate. She could not skip or even slide her feet along the floor. They felt as if they were glued in place. This bothered Vicki a great deal as she loved to dance. But she had to put it out of her mind, at least temporarily, as she had a date tonight and Bob was coming soon to pick her up.

Vicki had picked out a pair of cream coloured pants and a matching loose flowing, silk blouse. She topped the outfit with a gold sequinned jacket, gold coloured sandals and clutch. Bob picked her up at six and they drove to the Four Seasons Hotel, where Bob was staying. He had made a reservation at their Café Boulud because of its French cuisine. Vicki thought he was trying to recreate their trip to Paris, since they both enjoyed it so much. They had a lovely evening.

"Mark is really enjoying his new position in Atlanta. He is in charge of a twenty person sales team. I think he is very pleased."

"I am so happy for Mark, I will let Joanne know, as I am sure she will be interested."

Actually, Vicki knew she was very interested as she was carrying Mark's baby. But, of course, it was not her place to say anything.

"How is your job, Vicki?"

"Oh, it is just great, Joanne and I have been to Paris, as you know, and we just returned from Milan."

"It must be exciting to be able to travel to such interesting places and get paid for it."

"It really is exciting. I can't imagine doing any other job."

They enjoyed chicken cordon bleu and a bottle of Sauvignon Blanc. Vicki was having dinner with Bob, a perfect gentleman, but she could not stop thinking about Tom and wished it was Tom across the table from her.

Vicki thanked Bob for the lovely evening as he drove her home. She told him they could never be anything more than friends. He was very disappointed but kissed her on the cheek and said he would e-mail her when his business trip was over. Vicki agreed and went inside.

Barb heard her arrive home and she went over.

"Well, popular one, how was your date tonight?"

"He is very nice but all I can think about is Tom."

"Then, I think you should give Tom a call and let him know you are home and that you are thinking about him."

"Thanks, Barb, that is a great idea and furthermore, Tom's voice will be the last one I hear before I go to sleep. You are a genius, Barb."

When Tom answered the phone, he sounded so sad, but as soon as he heard Vicki's voice, he suddenly perked up and seemed much happier.

"I just called to let you know that I am home and thinking about you."

"Thank you so much Vicki; I was worried about some competition."

"Tom, you have no competition. I told Bob we could be nothing more than friends."

Every weekend after that, Vicki stayed at Tom's house. They went shopping together on Saturdays. They had dinner either at home or sometimes they would go to a restaurant. Vicki preferred to eat at Tom's home because they could have a barbeque, but, sometimes they would go out to a restaurant. Vicki liked eating at home not only because of the barbeque but because it was just the two of them and that felt wonderful. Sometimes they would go to the cinema or a live stage show. They would go to the market on Saturday and buy all their fresh vegetables and fruit for the following week. They took in trade shows when the shows were in Toronto and they even went to Fallsview Casino a couple of times. Casino Rama had some good entertainers in their theatre as well and they visited there occasionally.

All in all they just enjoyed being together.

CHAPTER 29

BIRTH OF JOANNE'S BABY

Then, Vicki had to make another buying trip; this time to London, England. Vicki's feet still felt heavy and she had started stubbing her toe when she walked. But, again she had to just put her symptoms aside in favour of doing her job.

Vicki was making this trip alone as Joanne was almost due to have her baby. As it turned out, the day before Vicki was to leave for London, she got a call from Joanne.

"Vicki, I am not sure, but I think I might be in early labour."

"Just sit quietly, Joanne, and I will be there in fifteen minutes to help you."

When Vicki arrived at Joanne's house, she could tell that Joanne was in labour. Vicki helped Joanne to the car and drove her to the hospital. When they arrived at the Emergency Department and Joanne was ushered to her room, Vicki said:

"Who would you like me to call for you?"

"Could you please call Bill, his number is in my purse."

"Okay, anyone else?"

Joanne's family lived in Florida so she said she would call them after the baby was born so she could give them the details.

"Oh, wait a minute. Mark was visiting his Dad in Toronto for a week. Bob had been in Toronto, on business, for the past month. He was setting up a new computer system in a downtown hospital and had to stay to make sure everything was working well before returning home to Ottawa. I told Mark about the baby and he wants to be here for the birth. Could you please call Mark and tell him?" said Joanne.

"Of course, I would be happy to call them."

Vicki left the room for a few minutes and made the calls. When she returned to Joanne's side, Joanne was in active labour.

Bill arrived soon after and held Joanne's hand and helped her with her breathing through the contractions.

When Joanne was almost fully dilated and the baby was imminent, Mark rushed into the room. He was very excited to be able to watch and help with the birth of his first child.

Bill stepped aside and let Mark help Joanne as it was their love child.

Bill and Joanne had previously discussed with Mark the fact that he would always be welcome in his child's life. Joanne and Bill were living together now so when Mark asked Joanne to join him in Atlanta, she very politely declined.

After Mark's arrival, following a few tiring minutes for Joanne, their baby daughter was born. She weighed seven pounds, seven ounces and was perfect. Mark and Joanne hugged and kissed through their tears as Vicki and Bill left the room to give them their privacy.

When Vicki returned to Joanne's room the nurse asked her if she would like to hold the baby. Vicki would have liked nothing better but she refused as she was feeling a bit unsteady with her balance and was afraid she might drop the child. Instead she just took pictures of Joanne, Mark and the baby.

CHAPTER 30

LONDON, ENGLAND

Vicki had never been to London and was looking forward to seeing Buckingham Palace and the Changing of the Guards. This trip, Vicki had to go alone as Joanne was in the hospital with her new daughter.

Vicki went to the bank to get British Pounds and to tell Tom about her trip as she had to leave the next evening, Tuesday, but would be home on Sunday morning.

In their meeting, before she left the office, it was decided to add a tweed suit and some skirts, so Vicki knew what she was looking for. Thursday and Friday were busy days for Vicki, looking at fashions for the fall line.

Saturday was a free day so Vicki decided to look for a fall coat. She went to a mall and passed a lingerie shop. It was quite large and had a beautifully designed window display. The nighties in the window caught her eye and again she was thinking about how Tom would like to see her in one of them. She decided to go into the store and admired all the lingerie on the main floor. There was a lovely collection of bras and matching panties, P.J.'s, robes and even bathing suits, but the nighties were on a floor about ten steps above the rest of the store. Vicki immediately went upstairs to check out the lovely silk nighties. She found one that she liked and headed down to the main floor to find a salesgirl to help her find the correct size. There were no railings on the stairs so she was being very careful, but nevertheless, she fell backwards and slid down the stairs. Several customers and sales staff came rushing over to help her to get up.

"Thank you, I am okay, it is just my arthritis," she said.

Vicki didn't even have arthritis but, in her embarrassment, that was all she could think of to say. She was not hurt and she left the store in shame and with no nightie.

Vicki flew out of Heathrow Airport on Saturday night to return to Toronto but did not tell anyone about her fall. She was too embarrassed.

CHAPTER 31

VICKI

On Monday morning Vicki went to see her doctor. The doctor checked her over and took her blood pressure. She also ordered a series of blood tests. Vicki had always had trouble with blood tests. Ever since she was a child, there were no visible veins in her arms. This made it very difficult for a lab technician to find a vein and draw blood. In the past, Vicki had ended up with bruises on her arms and both hands from having blood taken. Over the years Vicki had discovered that if the lab technician used a very small needle called a paediatric butterfly she could usually get the blood with no bruising.

Vicki made sure to inform the lab of this fact before the technician started to draw the blood. This method did work and Vicki was able to have the tests completed.

A few days later the doctor's office called and Vicki went in hoping to find an answer to her problem. When she sat in the doctor's office, the doctor said everything was normal. She must have just slipped. Vicki accepted her diagnosis, with a little scepticism, and went home.

The next day one of Vicki's girlfriends had invited Vicki and three other ladies for a poolside lunch. It was a bright, sunny day and Vicki was quite excited to join her friends for lunch.

When Vicki arrived at her friend's house the other ladies were already there. They each helped themselves to a glass of strawberry punch and took it outside to a table by the pool. There were three, wooden steps leading down from the deck to the pool area. As Vicki walked down the steps she, all of a sudden, sat down on the step, spilling her drink on the ground. One of her friends helped her up from this mysterious fall.

The rest of the luncheon was fun and the food was delicious. The ladies shared several stories of things they had been doing since they were last together. The friends enjoyed each other's company.

One morning, a few weeks later, Vicki was getting ready for work. Charlie had dropped in for an early coffee. Vicki was in the shower when Charlie arrived so he let himself in and started making the coffee. All of a sudden he heard Vicki call out. He ran to the bathroom door to ask what was wrong. Vicki was on the floor. She had fallen when she exited the shower and could not get back up. Charlie was hesitant to enter as he did not want to see his mother naked.

Vicki said: "Come in Charlie, I have a towel."

Charlie entered and got behind his mother and lifted her to her feet.

"Are you okay, Mom? If anything is broken I will take you to the hospital."

"I think I am fine, I don't know what happened. I will get dressed and we can talk over coffee."

Vicki had been having trouble getting in and out of her bathtub to take a shower for a while. There was nothing for her to hold onto when getting in and out of the tub and she was afraid that she would fall again. Because she lived alone she had to make sure she was safe from falls.

"I think I will call a handyman to come in and install a safety bar for me in the shower."

When the handyman arrived he installed two bars in Vicki's shower. He also mentioned that Vicki could purchase a set of two handles that attach to the shower by suction. Vicki ordered two sets of these handles. One set she would take to Tom's house and the other she would take with her when she travelled.

Vicki was also having difficulty getting up from the toilet. At home she would pull herself up by holding onto the counter. Whenever she went out and had to use a public washroom she always tried to get the handicap stall as there was a bar to hold onto that would help her get up. When Vicki was visiting friends or when she was at Tom's house she would take her purse into the bathroom with her and put the strap of her purse over the door handle and use the purse to pull herself up.

When Vicki mentioned this to her handyman, he suggested that she have a higher toilet installed in her bathroom so that she could get up easier. Vicki agreed and the new toilet was installed.

CHAPTER 32

AT TOM'S HOUSE

Vicki was staying at Tom's and they got up early Saturday morning and were at the Home Show at the Exhibition by ten a.m. They toured three model homes that were really more like cottages with two bedrooms, two baths, combination living and dining rooms and galley kitchens. Not something Tom or Vicki would be interested in. The flower displays, on the other hand, were magnificent; one in particular had small containers mounted all the way up a brick wall with some of the blossoms cascading down the wall. It was a display worth taking pictures of although Vicki knew she could never even attempt to duplicate it.

They were back home by three o'clock.

"Would you like to sit outside on the deck for a while before dinner?" Tom asked.

"I'd love to but we better put on warm sweaters, there is a chill in the air."

"You can put on the kettle and make us a hot chocolate to help keep us warm. I will go to the bedroom and get our sweaters."

"I love to sit outside and look at the trees and flowers, it is so beautiful." Vicki said.

"It is beautiful and much nicer with you here to share it with me," Tom replied.

They watched the neighbour's little Jack Russell terrier through the back fence. He was jumping around and playing with a ball that his owner was bouncing. Vicki loved dogs but couldn't have one in the condo where she lived. Actually, dogs were allowed but she couldn't see herself going out alone at night to walk a dog, since she was having difficulties with walking which included stubbing her toe and shuffling her feet. She would never be able to keep up with an active dog. She often thought about getting a cat but hadn't done so yet. She would probably get one sometime in the future when she was not travelling as much. Vicki loved animals as they were such good company.

By five thirty they were both feeling hungry, so they went inside to prepare dinner.

"Do you like Shake and Bake chicken?" Tom asked.

"Yes with rice and some vegetables?" Vicki added.

"How about broccoli with cheese sauce?"

"Sounds perfect and with a little side salad."

"What can I do to help?" Vicki asked.

"I can handle the kitchen if you can set the table."

Vicki started to set the table in the sunroom as she didn't want to mess up the beautiful dining room. She had just put the plates on the table and was sorting out the silver when all of a sudden, and for no apparent reason, she fell backwards and landed flat on her back. Tom heard her fall and came running into the sunroom.

"Are you okay dear? What happened?"

"I don't know what happened, I just fell. I was setting the table and the next thing I knew I was on the floor. I am so sorry, Honey, but I am okay."

Vicki didn't lose consciousness and didn't hurt herself. Tom helped her up and sat her in a chair for a few minutes. She insisted that she was fine and they continued with their dinner. Tom made her promise that she would see the doctor on Monday.

CHAPTER 33

NEUROLOGIST APPOINTMENT

On Monday morning, as promised, Vicki went to her doctor's office. The doctor examined her thoroughly and ordered more blood tests. All the reports came back normal. Vicki insisted something was wrong but the doctor could not find it so she referred Vicki to a neurologist. This was just neurologist number one, but Vicki did not know this at the time.

Vicki went into the neurologist's office and he asked her a lot of questions, the first being:

"How much do you drink?"

Vicki was insulted as she did not drink aside from an occasional glass of wine when she went out for dinner. She never drank at home on her own but the doctor was just doing his job as he didn't know her. After a number of questions, he asked her to sit up on his examination table and he tested her reflexes. They all seemed fine. He sent her for some more blood tests and a computed axial tomography (CAT) scan and also an electroencephalogram (EEG). This was the first time Vicki had had either of these tests. The EEG test took thirty minutes to perform. The test was painless and multiple electrodes were placed on her scalp to record her brain activity.

Vicki drove herself to the hospital. She drove around and around the parking lot looking for a place to park. They were all taken. Vicki considered going to another lot but when she arrived at the exit gate she found that she would have to pay eight dollars in order to open the gate for her to leave. Therefore, Vicki just drove around the parking lot, along with three other cars, all waiting to park. Vicki kept looking at her watch as she did not want to be late and miss her appointment. It was a lucky thing that she left her home twenty minutes earlier than she needed to for the drive to the hospital. She used ten minutes driving around waiting for a spot which finally became available when a motorcycle pulled out and left the parking lot.

When she arrived for her appointment in the Radiology Department of the hospital she was asked to change into a hospital gown and sit in the waiting room until she was called. She was then taken into a small room where she had to lie on a table. This table moved into a large cylinder where a number of x-rays were taken to form a 3-D image of her brain. This was completely painless as the machine did not touch her. In about half an hour she was finished and on her way home.

Vicki waited for a week thinking the doctor would discover her problem and all would be well again. When she went into his office, he asked her to take a seat and she figured it must be serious. She was very nervous and just wanted this appointment to be over. Then the doctor said:

"Everything is normal; I cannot find any problems in your blood work, the CAT scan or the EEG."

This upset Vicki a great deal as she was starting to feel very unsteady on her feet and was also starting to have a lot of trouble understanding what was said to her.

She was becoming confused by the instructions for cooking and baking, both of which she loved to do. Vicki was usually very cognizant. Her family and friends had noticed the difference and they started to wonder if Vicki was becoming a hypochondriac, as all her doctors said there was nothing wrong. Vicki was not usually a complainer but now just about everything bothered her.

Vicki's family also wondered if she was just looking for attention.

CHAPTER 34

NEW YORK CITY

The following month Vicki was scheduled to go to New York on another buying trip. By this time Vicki was feeling very shaky and her balance was getting unsteady. She was shuffling her feet rather than picking them up when she walked. She had tripped a few times always with her right toe but didn't fall. Instead of her sexy high heeled shoes she was wearing what she called *old lady flats*.

At work the stairs were right next to Vicki's office but she would walk all the way down the hall, past five or six other offices, until she reached the elevator. Vicki had a lot of trouble walking down stairs. She had to hold on to the railing and she still felt that she could fall. Since GFC was on two floors there were a number of trips from one floor to the other required each day. Vicki found that she was losing a considerable amount of time walking to the elevator. She sometimes skipped her lunch or breaks in order to make up the lost time.

"I sure do not feel sexy anymore, I just feel old."

Vicki and Joanne's maternity leave replacement, Betty, left for New York on Friday and were returning on Tuesday. They had a fashion show Friday evening and a meeting with buyers Monday morning.

As they were picking up their messages at the desk, in the hotel, Vicki suddenly fell backwards again. There was no warning, Vicki did not feel dizzy or uneasy. She just, all of a sudden, landed on her back. "How embarrassing, it happened in the lobby of a very large hotel." This time the hotel staff wanted to send her to the hospital but she refused as they were not in Canada and Vicki was sure she could wait until she got back. Betty was quite worried and took good care of her on the way home. She wouldn't let Vicki carry her own suitcase. Betty used a cart and pushed all of their bags herself. Vicki promised to see her doctor, once more, on her return.

CHAPTER 35

LEAVING GFC
(GREAT FASHION CHOICE)

On arrival in Toronto on Tuesday, Vicki made another appointment with her doctor who, she thought by now, must have been fed up seeing her. Vicki told her that she was thinking of taking early retirement as she could no longer function in the capacity for which she was hired. Vicki was then given a referral to a doctor who assessed patients for Government disability payments. She had to wait two weeks for this appointment and had to drive over an hour to his office, park a block away and climb a long flight of stairs to finally reach the office. If she wasn't tired when she started, Vicki sure was by the time she reached the office. This seemed very inappropriate to Vicki, for a doctor assessing a patient for a disability to be on the second floor of a building without an elevator. It was quite difficult for her and she was extremely nervous about going back down. When she got to the office and was sitting on his examination table Vicki heard that question again:

"How much do you drink?"

She felt like saying:

"Very little, I spill most of it."

But as this was no joking matter, she kept her comments to herself. The doctor then tested her reflexes starting with her feet, ankles and knees. He then tested the reflexes in her elbows. The doctor put an instrument into Vicki's ears to check them as balance is partially determined by the ears. He found nothing wrong with her so he disallowed the claim. Now Vicki had to carefully maneuver those stairs again.

"I guess if the doctor can't find the problem, then it doesn't exist," thought Vicki.

After much thought and discussion with Tom, Vicki took sick leave from the job that she loved. She would miss all her co-workers as they had become part of her life. She had a little money put aside following her divorce from Joe and GFC would put her on long term sick benefits. She would have to cut her expenses but it did help that whenever she went out with Tom, he paid for the evening. She knew that she would be okay financially and could concentrate on getting better.

Vicki went into John's office and told him she was ill and would have to leave her position. John was quite upset as he liked Vicki and her work. They discussed her situation and Vicki agreed to train a replacement before she left. Vicki suggested Betty, the girl who had replaced Joanne when she was on her maternity leave. John decided Betty would be a good replacement as she had already made one trip with Vicki.

CHAPTER 36

GETTING A CANE

Vicki had difficulty walking, was tripping and her balance was very poor so she decided to purchase a cane to help her walk. Vicki was visiting her local mall one day and she felt so unsteady. She was walking through the mall, looking in the store windows but she felt she had to walk close to a wall in case she lost her balance. She kept thinking that she could fall at any time. She was very nervous as she did not want to embarrass herself the way she had done in London when she fell down the stairs in the lingerie shop. So Vicki went into a drug store for some help and noticed that they had a number of canes. She stopped to look at them and a salesgirl came over to assist her.

"My balance is very poor and I feel unsteady. I feel as if I could fall at any time, Vicki told the sales girl.

"I think that a cane may be of help to you. May I help you select one?"

Vicki was embarrassed to have to use a cane so she picked the prettiest one she could find with flowers and butterflies. But it was still a cane.

"I will adjust the cane to fit your size," the salesgirl said.

"Just hold the cane as if you are using it and I will push the button on the cane and set it for you."

"It is important that you feel comfortable and we do not want to cause any back problems."

Vicki left the store with a little help for her wavering gait.

After she left the drug store, Vicki found carrying her purse in one hand and the cane in the other hand left her no possibility to carry shopping bags. Vicki then went into a luggage store as they had a terrific selection of handbags. She looked at a number of lovely, leather bags and with a little assistance from the salesgirl Vicki chose a crossover bag. This bag had a strap that crossed right over Vicki's chest so she did not need to use her hands to carry it. She felt very happy with this style of purse as she now had one hand free for carrying other things.

Through all of this, Tom was wonderful. He took her grocery shopping every weekend, they went to movies, shows and dinner. He even insisted that they take a holiday to a warm destination once a year. Tom talked about making things permanent between them but as much as Vicki would have loved to marry Tom, she could not commit as she was not well, and she knew it.

"Tom deserves more than a sick wife to look after; he needs someone to have fun with, to walk, hike, travel and dance with and I can no longer do any of these things."

Charlie took Vicki to all of her medical appointments from this time on as he was self-employed and could arrange his schedule to do this for his mom. Vicki had lost all confidence in driving her car and was having a lot of trouble with every-day living. She had trouble cleaning her condo and preparing her meals, so she ate a lot of frozen dinners that she could pop into the microwave. Weekends at Tom's house was such a treat as he made wonderful meals for them.

At one point Charlie and Vicki discussed the possibility of her having to go into a nursing home. Her life would have been over if she had chosen that course. After Vicki's very disturbing discussion with Charlie, she returned to her doctor and persisted in driving her crazy asking for another referral.

"Someone has to find the problem. I have been healthy all my life, and I take no medication so I know there is a problem. But what is it?"

Vicki knew her doctor was getting frustrated, but not as frustrated as she was getting.

By this time, Vicki was just sitting around the house most of the time as she was afraid to go out alone. On weekends Tom took her out and helped with her shopping. Because Vicki was spending so much time watching television, eating unhealthy foods and not exercising, she was rapidly gaining weight and this made her very unhappy.

Hence neurologist #2.

CHAPTER 37

VICKI'S BIRTHDAY

The weekend before Vicki's appointment with the second neurologist, it was her birthday. Maggie and George had invited her to a murder mystery dinner theatre. Tom was not able to join them that evening as he was the speaker at a Rotary Club dinner.

Maggie and George picked Vicki up but she had difficulty climbing into their SUV and when she got in Maggie had to fasten her seatbelt for her. They drove downtown. George parked the car and they walked to the theatre. Vicki was really looking forward to this evening as she had never been to a murder mystery dinner before, but as soon as she entered the theatre she panicked. There were thirty stairs going straight down to the theatre. It took Maggie and George several minutes to convince Vicki to go down these stairs. She only agreed if George took her arm and helped her maneuver the stairs while Maggie walked in front of Vicki to catch her if she fell.

When Maggie and George booked the dinner, they had mentioned that it was Vicki's birthday. Upon arrival, the waiter told George that Vicki would be called up to the stage to participate in the show. George explained Vicki's problem and she was given a small part so that she could remain at her table.

The dinner was delicious and the show was very amusing. George even solved the murder and received a hat as a prize.

When Vicki, Maggie and George eventually left the theatre and walked to the car, it took Vicki ten minutes to get into George's SUV as Vicki could not step up that high. Maggie had to give her a boost up to the seat. When she got into the car she could not figure out how the seatbelt worked and Maggie had to buckle her in again.

CHAPTER 38

NEUROLOGIST #2

The following week Vicki visited the second neurologist hoping he could solve the problem. As Charlie and Vicki entered the mall, where this doctor had an office on the second floor, they walked up to an escalator to take them upstairs. Charlie got on first and when Vicki followed, the escalator seemed to be moving too fast for her and she stumbled and started to fall backwards. One of the mall security guards saw what was happening and he caught her before she could fall. Charlie and Vicki were then directed to the elevator.

This doctor did all the same tests as the first neurologist but he added testing for Alzheimer's disease as she was losing her memory very quickly. She could not even tell her sister the ages of Emma and Susan, her only nieces. When Maggie would phone Vicki and ask her a question like; "did you shop yesterday," Vicki would just say, "I don't remember." Her conversations consisted of very few words.

The doctor also ordered tests for Parkinson's disease as Vicki could not walk properly; her balance was very unsteady.

Vicki told the doctor that she had already had two bouts of incontinence. Although she was aware that there were products available to protect her from embarrassment, she was very hesitant to use them. She just kept hoping it would not happen again. She could not explain the reason for the incontinence so she cut down on the water she was drinking and visited the bathroom often but to no avail; the problem continued.

Vicki had to wait two weeks for the results of her tests, but when Charlie took her back to the doctor, the doctor said:

"All your tests are normal. You do not have Alzheimer's nor do you have Parkinson's."

"Then what do I have because I know there is something seriously wrong going on in my body?"

"I hate to tell you this but since all your tests are normal and nothing is showing up, it must just be old age."

Imagine at age fifty five being told your symptoms are due to old age.

"**NO**, I refuse to believe that diagnosis."

CHAPTER 39

WORKING IN THE GARDEN

The weekend came and on Friday night Tom said:

"Would you like to go for a walk and stop in at an Italian restaurant that I know?"

"Is it very far? Because I have a problem walking any distance."

"Just about ten minutes and I will hold your arm and with your cane in the other hand, I promise you will be fine."

They walked slowly to the restaurant and enjoyed a delicious spaghetti dinner with garlic bread and a glass of Baco Noir. They sat for about two hours and then went window shopping along Mt. Pleasant that led back to Tom's street. Then they returned home.

The next day Vicki was staying at Tom's house and they decided to do some clean-up in the garden. Vicki had always loved working in the garden, especially cutting the grass. She plugged in the lawn mower but was unable to make it move. Tom took over and Vicki decided to trim the hedge at the front of the house. She felt wonderful and so energized being out in the fresh air. When the hedge clippings started to pile up Vicki went into the house to get some brown paper garden bags to hold the debris that had accumulated on the lawn. As Vicki was walking back to the front of the house, she tripped on the sidewalk that ran alongside the house to the front. Vicki landed on her face this time. Tom heard her and came running to help. Vicki was a dead weight and Tom, even though he was quite strong, had a difficult time lifting her to a nearby bench. Vicki was so weak that she could not even help herself to get up. Tom sat beside her for a few minutes as she was very shaky after the fall.

"Did I break my teeth?" was all Vicki asked.

"No Dear, your teeth are fine."

Ten minutes later, Vicki and Tom went into the house to clean Vicki's face. She was very upset when she looked in the mirror to see what had happened. Her lip was swollen and bleeding from a large cut in it. There were scrapes and bruises on her face. Tom washed her face and put some antibiotic cream on the scrapes and cuts. Vicki was worried about her looks as there was a barbeque at Maggie and George's house the next day and there would be a lot of people there.

Tom finished cleaning up outside while Vicki had a rest. After dinner, Tom said:

"Let's go out in the car and I will take you to a drug store to see what we can do with make-up before the barbeque."

"Oh, thank you, Tom, that would be wonderful as I would feel very self-conscious with my face looking like this."

Tom took Vicki to a large Shopper's Drug Mart in the area. He took her to the cosmetician and explained their problem. Together they picked a shade of cover-up that matched Vicki's skin and would cover the marks well. Tom purchased the make-up and Tom and Vicki returned to his house.

The following day Tom helped Vicki with the cover-up and they went to the party. Vicki's swollen lip was still evident but the scrapes and bruises were hidden. She felt reasonably comfortable with her appearance even though several people mentioned her swollen lip to her.

CHAPTER 40

TRIP TO ARUBA

On a very cold February evening Vicki sat watching television and she decided that the next day she would go shopping for some wool to knit an afghan. She had made baby outfits, sweaters for Charlie and herself, and even a bedspread, so now she decided on an afghan. Vicki checked her file of patterns and she found one that was not too difficult. She also found the correct sized needles.

"Tomorrow, I will go to the wool store and buy what I need to make this pattern," Vicki thought.

The next morning Vicki went out to the wool store and she bought enough blue and white wool, all in the same dye lot, to make the afghan she had chosen. Vicki carefully and slowly drove home quite excited to have a project to keep her busy.

When Vicki got home she took out the pattern and the needles and went into her living room to sit in a comfortable chair and begin her knitting. Vicki had to cast on one hundred and thirty stitches which she managed with minimal difficulty, but when the pattern said K2, P2 to the end of the row Vicki just sat there and looked at the needles and wool. She had no idea what this simple pattern meant. Vicki gave up in frustration and put the knitting away.

"Oh, how frustrating."

Tom called and told her he had just booked a trip for them to a warm destination, sunny Aruba, for ten days.

Because of her mobility problems, Vicki didn't want to go away but Tom insisted that she needed the warmth and he promised to take care of her.

The following week they left for the Resort in Palm Beach, Aruba. At the airport they checked their bags and headed down towards the departure gate. They no sooner started down the long corridor when a lady driving a golf cart came up to them and offered them a ride. She said it was a long way and since Vicki was using a cane it would take her too long to reach the gate. They were driven right to their gate and were first to board the plane. Using a cane does have some advantages. Probably the airport security would insist that disabled individuals were driven to their departure gate for safety reasons. Vicki admitted that she felt old and crippled accepting this needed help. She would give anything not to need help and to be able to walk to the gate independently.

Tom and Vicki arrived at the resort in the middle of the afternoon. They went to the reception desk to check in and were given a suite on the third floor. This resort had several three storey units and there were no elevators. Tom explained that they needed to be on the ground floor as Vicki could not walk down stairs.

They had to wait for about an hour for the manager to switch their room as the resort was full but he eventually found them a suite on the lower level with no stairs.

They spent the rest of the day discovering where everything was located. The resort had five restaurants, a huge pool, three hot tubs and, of course, a casino. For dinner they went to the buffet. Tom walked with Vicki as she chose her food. Then he carried her plate to the table before he went back to get his dinner. They went to see the show that the staff put on every evening. It was fun with lots of dancing and singing. The girls wore lovely dresses in beautiful colours and the men wore fancy, brightly coloured vests, shirts and pants. Vicki took lots of photos as that was the one thing she could still do.

The next day they just sat by the pool. They were tired from the trip so decided to take it easy that day. They both put on their bathing suits and a lot of SPF 30 sunscreen as their skin was not used to the rays of the hot sun in Aruba. Then they headed down to the pool and Tom got two lounge chairs for them and they sat side by side for a couple of hours. Tom wanted them to go for a swim but Vicki didn't feel confident enough to venture in, so Tom went alone and she just watched.

By the third day they were ready to have some fun. They spent the day at the pool and after an early dinner went to the casino. They tried their luck at a few different games. Vicki only played the slot machines as there was too much money involved with the table games. She could play the slots with a twenty dollar bill. Vicki lost twenty dollars but Tom won two-hundred dollars, so all was well.

The next evening they decided to go dancing. There was a dance after a beach barbeque at their resort. They found a table and were soon joined by another couple, from British Columbia, who looked about their age. They became friends that evening and met for cocktails before dinner, most nights after that. When Vicki made it to the dance floor on Tom's arm the music was playing Marc Anthony's *Tu Amor Me Hace Bien,* a very beautiful Latin love song. But she could not pick her feet up, so she just shuffled around the dance floor. One dance was all she could handle as her legs ached so much and they sat the rest of the dances out. When they returned to their room Vicki started to cry. She loved to dance and she had always been a good dancer but now she was just an old lady who couldn't even dance. Tom comforted her; they made love before finally going to sleep.

By the fourth day they decided to go down to the beach instead of the pool. The sand looked so white against the green water and blue sky with not a cloud in sight. Vicki found it extremely difficult to walk in the sand as her balance was so poor. Her feet were sinking with every step. She had enough trouble on a flat floor so she found walking in the sand almost impossible. Again, Tom held her arm and they made it to the water. Vicki left her cane on the beach and held Tom's arm as they walked into the beautiful, warm, turquoise water. It turned out to be too much for her with the swirling of the water and she fell into the sea taking Tom with her. Even though her fall was no laughing matter, they were sitting there laughing so hard that they couldn't even get up. A lady came up and said:

"May I help you to get up?"

She had seen Vicki's cane on the beach and thought she could use some help as she was holding onto Tom so tightly that he couldn't move. Vicki accepted her offer of help and the very kind, young lady came into the water and extended her hand. She walked Vicki to the beach and gave her the cane. "Talk about feeling old and useless."

Tom soon joined Vicki on the beach and they proceeded back to their room.

On the way up the beach they stopped to talk to a man who was sitting in a lounge chair. He was staying in the suite next to theirs and Vicki and Tom had met him the day before. As they stood there talking, Vicki could feel her heels sinking. There was nothing she could do to save herself and she fell backwards. She was fine since she fell on sand. After Tom helped her up and they said their goodbyes to their new friend, he said to Tom:

"You know you shouldn't let your wife drink that much."

Vicki and Tom didn't explain, they just left. They went back to their suite to rest and shower before dinner.

The next day they agreed to stay at the pool as it was safer for Vicki. After sitting in the hot sun for a few hours they decided to get into the pool to cool off. They got in together with Vicki holding very tightly to Tom's arm. As soon as Vicki was in the water, she started to feel unsteady. Vicki would not let go of the side of the pool. More than likely, the movement of the water was causing her unsteadiness but Tom had to virtually carry her out as she was frozen to the side of the pool. Needless to say, for the rest of the vacation, Tom swam alone and Vicki watched from her chair.

"Oh, what fun! Sorry Tom."

The return trip home was very upsetting as well. On their arrival at Pearson International Airport, Vicki was offered a wheel chair. She already felt old with the cane but this was the worst. Of course Vicki refused the help and walked with her cane, stubborn as she was.

CHAPTER 41

MAGGIE AND GEORGE'S PARTY

A week after Vicki and Tom returned to Toronto, Maggie and George had an anniversary party. They had a large two-storey house. There were three stone steps leading up to the front door. Tom had to take Vicki's arm to help her up those steps and when they got into the foyer Tom had to help her take her shoes off. They entered the party but had to stay on the main floor. Vicki could not join in the activities downstairs in the recreation room as she couldn't manage stairs. Going downstairs was almost impossible. There were lots of Maggie and George's friends and also Vicki's friend whom she had known for almost twenty years. They had not seen each other for a couple of years and when the friend saw Vicki she couldn't believe her eyes. She said she did not even recognize her at first; Vicki looked so sick and helpless and she had gained a lot of weight.

Nevertheless, the party was fun and it was a pleasure to be with so many happy people instead of just doctors all saying she was normal. "SURE I WAS."

The next day as Vicki sat watching television as she very often did, the phone rang.

"Hello" said Vicki.

"Hi Vicki, what are you doing?" said Maggie.

"Nothing" was the answer Vicki gave.

"Did Charlie call you this morning?" Maggie asked.

"I don't remember."

"Have you been shopping this week?"

"I think so."

"What are you going to do today, Vicki?"

"I don't know."

"I will call you later," replied a frustrated Maggie.

CHAPTER 42

TALKING ON THE TELEPHONE

One afternoon when Vicki was alone at home her phone rang. It was her friend, Karen, who lived in Peterborough. They were talking for a while and then, all of a sudden, Vicki fell backwards onto the kitchen floor. Karen was terrified:

"Should I call 9 1 1?"

"I don't even know what to tell them."

"Oh, I wish I was closer so I could go over and help her."

"I know Vicki is alone and I am afraid for her safety."

Vicki was able to reach the phone and she assured Karen that she was okay and told her to wait a couple of minutes so she could pull herself up to her feet. This she managed to do and they finished their conversation with Vicki sitting on a chair and putting Karen's mind at ease.

Vicki had a couple more falls at home, one when she hit her face on the night table as she was getting into bed. She cut her cheek and there was another cut just above her left eye. As it was her face, the bleeding was quite profuse and her nightie was a mess. Vicki was alone so she called Charlie as she knew he was not too far away. Charlie and Annie were visiting friends and they went over and offered to take Vicki to the hospital. As she was already in bed and bandaged when they arrived, she said she would see her doctor in the morning. Charlie and Annie were reluctant to leave her without medical help but she assured them that she was fine and they went home. They instructed her to call them if anything happened, or if she felt unwell or frightened, and to see the doctor the next day. This she did. The doctor said Vicki should have had stitches after the fall, but now she would use some tape to close the cut on her cheek and Vicki was to return in one week for the doctor to check it.

When Vicki returned in a week, she again asked for another referral. Vicki knew her doctor felt she was just grasping at straws and Vicki could tell by the look on her doctor's face that she was running out of ideas. Because Vicki had requested the referral, her doctor was compelled to find yet another neurologist.

Hence neurologist #3.

CHAPTER 43

NEUROLOGIST #3

Vicki had to wait four weeks for the appointment with this neurologist. Charlie arrived a little early that day and had a cup of coffee with her before they got into his little blue sports car for the ride to Vicki's appointment. Vicki asked Charlie to go into the office with her to talk to the doctor as her comprehension had become progressively worse and although she could hear what was being said, she had trouble understanding the meaning. They entered the doctor's office, Vicki with her cane and Charlie by her side holding her arm, as she was very unsteady even with the cane. This doctor asked all the usual questions including that question that seemed to plague her every visit:

"How much do you drink?"

"I only drink wine, socially," Vicki said.

He then tested the reflexes in her elbows and knees. Vicki thought to herself that this is what every other doctor had done and nothing abnormal showed up. She was feeling very disappointed.

Then he did something the other doctors had not done. He took Charlie and Vicki through his waiting room and into the main hallway. It was a long carpeted hall with medical offices on either side. He asked Vicki if she could walk a little way down the hall, turn and walk back. She said:

"Okay"

Then he said:

"Give me your cane."

"Oh No!"

Vicki flatly refused to give it up. When she refused, the doctor asked why. Vicki said:

"My balance is so unsteady I am afraid I will fall." He agreed to let her use the cane. After this test they went back into the office and he ordered something else, that was new to Vicki; a test that Vicki had not had yet, an MRI.

Since this doctor's office was in the hospital she was able to have the MRI right away. Charlie took her downstairs to the Radiology Department and she was asked to undress and put on a gown. Then they brought a wheelchair to take her to the MRI room.

"Boy, do I feel old."

Vicki honestly thought that she would die very soon.

Vicki was now too weak to walk herself. Of course, she needed help to get up onto the table. The technician then put a basket-like contraption over her head and screwed it to the table. This was to prevent her head from moving during the test. It was a little daunting as she had no control. The table then moved and she was inside the machine. Vicki felt very nervous and a little claustrophobic. The machine was very noisy and there were cylinders revolving all the way around Vicki's body. The technician did explain the tests as they were going on over a loud speaker in the machine. This helped Vicki to relax as it was always better to know what to expect before it happened.

With the test completed, Charlie took her home. The technician had explained that an MRI, magnetic resonance imaging, is much like a CAT scan in that it is non-invasive to the patient. He said the MRI would give a much more detailed picture than x-rays or even CAT scans.

CHAPTER 44

THE DIAGNOSIS

A few days later Vicki received a call to come back to the doctor's office so he could give her the results of the tests. She was expecting him to tell her everything was normal. Charlie and Vicki returned to the doctor's office. The doctor invited them in and offered them seats as all the other doctors before him had done. Then he said the words that Vicki will remember for the rest of her life.

"I know what is wrong with you and you are not imagining it. You have a condition called NPH which is Normal Pressure Hydrocephalus or water on the brain."

Vicki thought that it was just babies who got hydrocephalus but she was wrong. The doctor explained to her that one in every two hundred adults over the age of 50 will get NPH. Unfortunately, this condition is not always diagnosed and patients have a progressive deterioration for the rest of their lives. Vicki knew she was very lucky and had done the right thing insisting on so many doctors' visits. She felt lucky to be alive and ready for whatever treatment the doctor suggested to help her condition.

"This doctor seems very cocky but I love him already," said a very excited Vicki.

"I am the diagnostician and I will send you to my mechanic," he said.

Vicki was then referred to a neurosurgeon at a very large hospital in Toronto. The thought of a brain surgeon should have scared her to death, but she was so relieved that her problem was finally diagnosed that she was thrilled to see this surgeon. Vicki could not believe that she had absolutely no fear of the surgery. She guessed it was because she was so relieved to finally have a diagnosis. She even surprised herself.

As soon as Vicki got home, she called Tom and told him she had a diagnosis, finally, and she was not imagining her illness. She had NPH. Vicki explained that her condition was Normal Pressure Hydrocephalus. She had an excess of the cerebrospinal fluid that circulates up and down the spine and around the brain. With the excess accumulation, there was pressure on the brain causing the symptoms she was experiencing. Tom was ecstatic that the problem had been identified and could be corrected. They discussed it for a few minutes and then Tom said:

"This deserves a celebratory dinner, my Dear, where would you like to go?"

"I think I feel like Italian. How about that new Italian restaurant just down the street? Barb was there and she said the food was terrific. I would love to try it."

"Wonderful, I will pick you up in an hour and congratulations Dear!"

CHAPTER 45

PREPARING FOR SURGERY

Charlie and Vicki saw the surgeon two weeks later. As they went in, Charlie held Vicki's arm and she had her cane in her other hand.

The doctor explained the procedure of inserting a VP (ventriculoperitoneal) shunt into her brain and down to her abdomen to drain the excess fluid. He then proceeded to book the surgery as soon as possible.

Vicki called Tom again and gave him the dates and explained the procedure to him. The next day Tom called her back and said:

"Vicki, I have just booked three weeks' vacation at the time of your surgery and I will come and stay with you as I know you will need some help."

"Thank you very much Tom, I am sure I will need lots of help but you shouldn't have to use your vacation to look after me."

"I want to do it and besides when you are well again we can travel together."

CHAPTER 46

VICKI'S SURGERY AND RECOVERY

On the day of surgery, Charlie drove Vicki to the hospital and Tom met them there. The three of them were directed to a large waiting room. There were ten other people there, some watching the television in one corner of the room. Others were reading one of the many magazines on the tables around the room. After about twenty minutes a nurse asked Vicki to follow her to a room where she was to be prepped for surgery. Vicki's two favourite men waited in the waiting room for her surgeon to tell them she was okay. After approximately five hours they received the news. They saw her in the recovery room and then left the hospital to return the next day to take her home.

The next day Charlie arrived at the hospital just after Tom. Vicki was anxious to go home but the nurse said she had to walk to the end of the hall and back using a walker before they would discharge her. It was difficult as she was very weak but with Tom on one side and Charlie on the other for moral support, Vicki managed the task and was discharged home. Tom drove her home as he was going to stay with her. Charlie had rented a walker and he took it over to her home. Arrangements had been made for a nurse to visit once a day to change the bandages. Vicki's hair had been partially shaved off on the right side of her head and this bothered her quite a bit. Physiotherapy would visit twice a week to try to get her back to a cane.

"Whoopi."

Vicki did all the exercises she was given very diligently as she was determined to regain her ability to walk. The first step was to get rid of the walker and use a cane. Tom stayed with her for 3 weeks and helped her shower, dress and he cooked the meals for them. By the time Tom left, Vicki was walking with a cane and was able to drive her car to outside physiotherapy. She went to this physiotherapy faithfully for three years. They started her out with simple stretching exercises and then she would lie on a moist hot pack for twenty minutes. This treatment progressed to more exercises for her legs, lifting and bending. She had to walk up and down three steps, several times during each treatment. Vicki was also given a maneuver where she had to roll a large exercise ball down the wall, holding it with her back. This was extremely difficult as it used the upper thigh muscles which in Vicki's case were weak. Then Vicki advanced to the treadmill. She also had to walk a straight line without stepping on the lines. The therapist then brought a chair in for Vicki and she had to sit and stand ten times without any help from her hands. She also had to stand facing the wall and go up on her tip toes and back down. This she did for ten repetitions.

Vicki was extremely happy to be confident again behind the wheel of her car and she felt a little independence returning to her life. She added two pound free weights to her ankles and lifted the same and finally had enough strength in her legs to get rid of the cane. Tom and Vicki celebrated by going dancing. Now Vicki was doing things she had not been able to do for a very long time.

"WOW I feel so good, I have to make up for lost time."

There was nothing Vicki would not try, walking long distances, what a pleasure, hiking, swimming even golfing.

CHAPTER 47

GETTING BACK TO NORMAL

After three years of physiotherapy, Tom booked Vicki and himself on a trip to Cayo Santa Maria, Cuba for 2 weeks. They had a wonderful trip and she enjoyed walking on the beach. She even walked in the water and the movement did not bother her one bit. Vicki was ecstatic. "I am back in the land of the living."

One day when they were on the beach, a vendor came along with two very large, beautiful parrots. He would allow someone to take a picture of another person with a bird on each of their arms. Before her surgery this would have been out of the question. But Vicki was eager to try. Tom was ready with the camera and the vendor placed the birds on her arms. Believe it or not, Vicki stood barefoot in the sand, the birds were heavy and her balance was perfect. She remembered when she could not even walk or stand in the sand. Vicki was so happy at her accomplishments that she had a grin on her face all day long. She could not believe how good she felt that she was no longer an invalid. Vicki felt so young again.

When they returned to Toronto, Vicki hosted a dinner party for Tom's brother and his wife. She made pork tenderloin in raspberry reduction, stuffed green, red and yellow peppers, but no potatoes as the peppers were stuffed with rice. They had home-made chocolate zucchini loaf and vanilla ice cream. Tom opened two bottles of wine, one white and one red and they sipped wine as they enjoyed their dinner. They finished off with a carafe of coffee. Vicki loved to host dinner parties for family and friends but for the past few years had been unable to do so. She had really missed this part of her social life as she liked to cook and to fuss over details and her guests.

The next few months were wonderful with lots of shopping trips and dinners out. Vicki and Tom toured gardens, museums and even went to Niagara Falls and took lots of pictures. Vicki was feeling back to her normal self. She enjoyed every trip they took remembering how difficult simple things used to be.

CHAPTER 48

TOM

Tom and Vicki had a date for dinner on Monday and when he did not show up, Vicki started to get worried.

"This is not like Tom at all."

She called his home but there was no answer, just his machine picked up. She left a message saying it was Vicki and she was worried about him. Then she sat in front of the T.V. but couldn't concentrate. She watched the news but didn't have any idea what she had heard. Then she decided to try a sitcom. After three of her favourites, she still could not stop thinking about Tom and she started pacing the floor. Vicki called Barb who came over right away and sat with her as she tried to breathe.

"I am sure he is alright, Vicki, try not to worry. He will call you soon."

"What if he was in an accident and can't call."

"I can't lose my Tom just when everything is starting to improve."

Barb made tea and tried to calm Vicki down but she was so worried. At around ten o'clock that evening the phone rang and it was a nurse from the trauma centre at a hospital located near Tom's bank. Tom was okay and ready to leave the hospital. He had been taken there by ambulance after a bullet grazed his leg earlier that afternoon during an attempted robbery at his bank.

Vicki took a deep breath and wiped the tears from her eyes and told Barb. Barb called her a cab. When Vicki arrived at the hospital, she entered the door leading into the Emergency Department. There were about eight or nine patients in the waiting area. Vicki went up to the desk and asked for Tom. She was directed through a door at the end of the hall and told to walk to the nurse's station and they would direct her further. She found Tom sitting in a chair ready to go home. Vicki sat with him for a minute or two and then they left the hospital.

They took another cab to his house and on the way Tom told Vicki that he was working in his office when a young man dressed in black from head to foot and wearing a black balaclava to disguise his face, came into the bank with a gun pointed at Tom's head teller. Luckily the teller was able to push the alarm button under her desk to alert the police. Tom took a gun out of a locked drawer in his desk.

Tom had taken a gun safety course a few years ago as part of his career training. The course consisted of two days of classroom instruction, and two days of range practice. After he had completed the instruction and practice shooting at targets, there was a three hour examination. This was a strict course and Tom passed with a ninety five percent average. Tom was given a license to carry a gun.

He quietly tip-toed around behind the robber and told him to drop the gun. The robber dropped it but not before he took a shot at Tom. The bullet hit the side of his left calf. It did not penetrate his leg but grazed the skin causing a six inch gash in his calf.

The police arrived on the scene and took the robber away in handcuffs. Fortunately the bullet had not entered Tom's leg but he did require stitches. He was then discharged from the hospital.

Vicki stayed with Tom that night to make sure he wasn't in shock and then she went home at noon on Tuesday but not before she had prepared a cheese and tomato sandwich with some cherries on the side for lunch. She then baked a meat loaf, potato and carrots for his dinner. Vicki also made custard with fresh raspberries on top. Tom took the rest of the week off work to recuperate. He was quite anxious to return to the bank but Vicki insisted he stay home for the week and he listened to her and took it easy.

CHAPTER 49

MORE PROBLEMS

Three and a half years following Vicki's surgery, she was visiting Charlie and Annie for a few days. Vicki had been feeling a little dizzy for a few weeks now and had been examined by her doctor and received an MRI. Nothing appeared abnormal, so Vicki figured it was just her allergies and she carried on.

On the way back home she was on the highway, driving by rote, and feeling a little confused. Vicki missed her exit and kept driving. When she finally realized what she had done she had no idea where she was or how to get home. Vicki decided to pull over to the side of the road and set her GPS. When she pulled off the road, in her confusion, she misjudged her car and scraped it all the way down the concrete barrier at the side of the road. Vicki had not only scratched the paint but she had dented the front fender of her brand new car. She managed to get home by following the instructions given by her GPS.

After Vicki got home, she called Tom to tell him of her accident. Tom said:

"Don't worry, Dear, I will look at it when I come over on Friday evening and we can make arrangements to have it repaired."

By Thursday of that week Tom started getting worried as he had not been able to get Vicki on the phone for a couple of days. They always talked on the phone every evening when

Tom returned home from work. They discussed what they did that day and their plans for the next day. Just to hear his voice made Vicki happy. When they had not spoken to each other for two days, and Tom could not reach her on the phone, he called Barb and asked her to check on Vicki.

Barb immediately went over to her suite. She knocked on the door and when there was no answer she used the key Vicki had given her and she opened the door. After calling Vicki's name a couple of times and receiving no reply she entered the suite. It was dark so Barb turned on the light in the hall. To her horror, Barb found Vicki unconscious on the bathroom floor. She was lying on her back, in the bathroom, and her new, very expensive nightie was soaked in urine. After calling 911, Barb called Tom who let Charlie know and they all met at the hospital. On arrival at the hospital Vicki was still unconscious and the paramedics were saying that she had had a stroke.

Barb, Tom and Charlie all said that Vicki had a shunt in her brain but the paramedics, being unfamiliar with NPH, still insisted it was a stroke and she remained unconscious overnight. After the Emergency physician had stabilized her, he called in a neurosurgeon to assess Vicki and, of course, he was familiar with shunts. The neurosurgeon inserted a very large needle into her skull and withdrew a small amount of fluid and she immediately woke up. It was discovered that the drainage tube had become blocked and fluid was accumulating in Vicki's brain again. Her previous neurosurgeon had not warned her that shunts could become blocked and need replacement. Hence a second surgery was necessary to replace the tubing. By this time it was early evening and Vicki was scheduled for surgery around midnight. Tom and Charlie were allowed to accompany Vicki to the pre-surgery room to keep her company until it was her turn. The anesthesiologist came in to see Vicki and she asked a number of questions, one was:

"What medications do you take?"

When Vicki told her that she did not take any medications, the anesthetist said:

"I love you; most patients come in with a long written list."

Soon after this, Vicki was pushed on her stretcher down a long hall and parked outside OR #3 waiting for her turn which came in about half an hour. This time Vicki was in hospital for 3 days and again went home with a walker. When Vicki arrived home and she and Tom were watching television she kept putting her hands to her head and saying:

"It is so noisy in here."

This continued for the next four days but Vicki knew it was the swelling in her brain from the surgery. The surgeon had told Vicki that this would go away as the swelling subsided. By the fourth evening as Vicki and Tom were watching television Vicki said, in a very surprised voice and with her hands on her head:

"Hey, it's quiet in here."

Tom took a week off to help her and after a week she was able to manage on her own. It was about a month to full recovery. It was much easier this time as she had been active up until the surgery. Vicki hated the walker so she worked very hard to get to a cane but she did not like that either as it made her feel old. Vicki worked even harder on her exercises until she was back to normal.

One thing that bothered Vicki a great deal was the fact that in order to have brain surgery a portion of her hair had been shaved off once again. She and her hairdresser figured out how to change her hair style in order to hide the shaved section which was just above her forehead on her right side. Vicki figured this was a very small price to pay to get her life back.

Finally Vicki was making up for the life she lost to NPH. She was even playing golf. Vicki and Tom were unable to travel for six months as she could not get travel insurance to leave the country following the surgery. She had to be stable for a minimum of six months before she was insurable.

CHAPTER 50

THE PROPOSAL

One evening, three months after the surgery, Tom took Vicki back to the Rainbow Suite where they had gone for their first date. He ordered a bottle of Grattamacco as he did on their first date. They sipped the wine and Tom took a small blue velvet box from his pocket.

Vicki knew what he was about to do and her heart started beating very fast. She was so excited. Vicki had hoped for this for a long time and now she was healthy and could enjoy what was about to happen.

"All my dreams are coming true. Who could have known that at this age I would be in love again."

Tom leaned across the table and gave her a kiss. He gazed into her eyes.

"Vicki, we have been so happy together taking trips and even staying home. I know you were worried when you were ill but now you are fine and I love you so much. Darling, will you marry me?"

Vicki thought her heart actually stopped beating and she could hardly breathe.

"Tom, my love, I would be so proud to be your wife. Yes, I will marry you."

Then Tom placed a magnificent, blue sapphire ring on Vicki's finger. It was a large blue stone surrounded by twelve large diamonds. Vicki felt so wonderful, as now she was well enough to accept his proposal and anticipate a healthy life together. They discussed a wedding date and decided on one in six months' time.

When Vicki told Barb how Tom had proposed and how excited she was, Barb was so happy for her. There was even a tear in her good friend's eye. Barb was so excited and offered to help Vicki with the plans and picking out the perfect dress. Tom said he would look after the honeymoon arrangements and he chose Hawaii for the honeymoon.

"Wonderful! I have never been there."

Tom chose the venue. It was a resort and spa at Keauhou Bay. The name means New Beginning. What a perfect place to start a new life together.

Vicki went over to Barb's suite one evening and they discussed different plans for a wedding.

A large wedding in Toronto and a honeymoon in Hawaii.

A small wedding with the honeymoon in Hawaii.

The honeymoon in Hawaii was the wonderful part of their plans. This was thanks to Tom.

Then Barb came up with the best suggestion of all—a destination wedding in Hawaii.

They planned a small, intimate wedding with twenty-two guests and the bride and groom making twenty-four. The guest list consisted of: Charlie and his wife Anne, Maggie and George, Emma and Susan. Barb and John as well as Joanne and Bill were also on the guest list. Tom's son Alex and his wife Bonnie, Tom's daughter Melissa her husband Brian and 2 sons, Justin and Raymond were invited. Tom's brother Martin and his wife Joan and Tom's 2 best friends Tony and Joseph and their wives Pat and Jane made up the twenty two guests. Maggie was to be Vicki's Maid of Honour and Tom's brother Martin was to be his best man.

CHAPTER 51

AT THE COTTAGE

Pre-wedding party with Tom's family and friends

Tom decided a weekend away with his brother, son and daughter and his best friends was a good idea so they could all enjoy time together before the wedding.

Tom rented a five bedroom cottage on Lake Simcoe at Brechin Beach. Vicki and Tom drove up Friday evening, past Lagoon City, turned left and drove past several cottages before they found the one that Tom had rented. It had two stories, with yellow siding and was right on the beach. They gave the five bedrooms to their guests and Tom and Vicki took a couch each in the family room. They had a television, fireplace and a very extensive library.

On Saturday morning after breakfast, they all did different activities from fishing, boating, swimming, and sitting in the sun to reading.

After lunch they decided to go for a long hike together through the various trails in the area.

"Everyone, grab a bottle of water to take with you," said Tom.

"There are some apples and bananas on the counter in the kitchen, help yourself."

They hiked for over four hours after which time they were all starving and getting tired.

When they got back to the cottage, Tom immediately started the barbeque.

"We have sirloin steaks for everyone but if you would like something else there are hamburgers and hot dogs in the fridge. Just bring them to me and I will cook them for you."

"I will make the potato salad," Vicki offered.

"Bonnie and I will make a nice green salad as I brought mixed salad greens, tomatoes and onions," said Melissa.

Then Joan offered:

"I will do the desserts. I brought cookies and two pies."

Pat and Jane were left to cut up the fruit.

"We will also set the table."

After dinner they sat around a huge bonfire on the beach roasting marshmallows on a stick from eight o'clock to well past midnight. They sang a lot of old camp songs, told some jokes and scary stories and really had a lot of fun. "What a nice way to enjoy Tom's family and friends."

Sunday morning they had a big breakfast of bacon, scrambled eggs, toast, waffles, juice and coffee.

Alex said: "Hey Dad! Bonnie and I are going to skip breakfast so we can take the canoe out before we go home."

"Okay, Alex but take a muffin and some fruit with you."

"See you in about an hour, Dad."

Then Alex and Bonnie got into the canoe and paddled out onto the lake. They were enjoying the open water and the peaceful quietness of early morning. They paddled past cottages belonging to movie stars and cottages that were rentals. The birds were singing and Alex was trying to identify them by their songs. Some were easy, like the cardinal and some were more difficult. Alex and Bonnie were singing as they paddled along. They were really enjoying the beautiful morning together and were not too anxious to return home to work the next day.

Just then, a motor boat sped past them. It was travelling at a very high speed and swerving about. Alex and Bonnie's canoe got caught in its wake. The little canoe they were in flipped over and they both plunged into the water. Alex came up immediately but Bonnie did not. He dove down and found her under the canoe. She must have hit her head and she appeared to be unconscious. Alex, having been a lifeguard when he was in his teens, managed to drag Bonnie to the shore. She had stopped breathing, at least it appeared so, and Alex started rescue breathing. After about a minute he heard a cough and Bonnie spit up a considerable amount of water.

"Oh sweetheart, are you okay?"

"I *cough* think *cough* so."

"I was so scared when you didn't surface after the canoe flipped over. You must have hit your head."

"Maybe I did because the top of my head hurts."

"Just lie still for a few minutes until I figure out what to do."

In the meantime Tom and Vicki were starting to worry.

"Tom, it has been two hours, is Alex usually on time?"

"Yes, I hope they are okay."

After another half hour Tom and Martin walked along the shore to see if they could see anything. Another half hour passed and they returned to the cottage.

"We had better call the police so they can go out in a boat to look for them," said Tom.

"I agree, would you like me to call?"

"Yes, thanks Vicki, I will go back down to the water's edge to watch for them."

The police arrived in about ten minutes in a speed boat and Tom and Martin got in with them to help find the canoe. They went quite a distance and were about to turn around when one of the officers spotted something red in the water. As they got a little closer to it they could see that it was an overturned canoe but no people were present. They pulled up alongside and Tom identified the canoe as the one Alex and Bonnie had gone out in.

"We have to search the nearby beaches," said the officer and they eased the boat a little closer to shore. In doing so, they could see a person waving frantically and yelling for attention.

"That looks like my son Alex, but where is Bonnie?" said Tom anxiously.

They pulled in closer and Tom jumped into the water and made it as quickly as possible to the shore. He found Alex in good shape but Bonnie was lying beside him and she looked very pale.

The two officers and Martin helped Tom get Bonnie into the boat. Alex followed and explained what had happened.

The police then took everyone back to their cottage with the canoe in tow. Bonnie was feeling better now, so Alex said he would stop in at the Orillia Hospital to have her checked out before returning home.

"Would you like Vicki and me to go to the hospital with you?"

"No thanks, Dad, I think we are fine. Bonnie looks better now, but just to be sure that she is out of danger we will have her examined by a doctor. I will call you when we get home."

"Take care then, son."

CHAPTER 52

PLANNING THE WEDDING

With the guest list completed, Barb and Vicki picked a lovely white embossed invitation from the craft store. There was a single white rose on the front of the card. These invitations came in a package of twelve and they had no writing inside. As Maggie had exquisite penmanship, she offered to write the invitations. Vicki and Tom were pleased to accept her generous offer.

Now it was time to find a dream dress. Barb and Vicki went downtown to several bridal shops.

In the first shop Vicki tried on four lovely gowns, the first was a blue dress with a lace and chiffon jacket. The dress had an empire waist which made her look quite slim. Vicki had dieted and lost the extra weight that she had gained when she was unable to exercise or even walk very far. She watched what she ate and had joined a weight loss group. Vicki walked for one hour every day and this proved very beneficial and she felt attractive now and enjoyed trying on dresses.

The next dress was also long and it was brown and had two straps on each shoulder exposing the shoulder itself.

Number three was just at the knee, a rose colour with ¾ sleeves and sequins all over the front of the dress. A little too fancy, Vicki thought.

Then number four; again it was long, a nice pastel pink and it had a wrap-style skirt.

They left this shop and ventured into several more.

Vicki tried a long taffeta dress with long sleeves but felt this would be far too hot for a wedding in Hawaii.

There was one dress that had five tiers in a short skirt. There was a little jacket to cover the sleeveless dress. Vicki quite liked this one.

She tried on two short dresses made of lace and they looked nice too.

She tried a twist front cocktail dress but this one made her look fat. After all the time and effort she had invested in getting into shape, she certainly did not want this dress.

Vicki finally chose a pink champagne dress in delicate cotton with a handkerchief hemline. The dress had spaghetti straps and it felt nice and cool and comfortable for a wedding in Hawaii. She found a pair of strappy shoes in the same champagne colour and "Guess what? I can finally wear heels again."

They were not too high; about two and a half inches.

"I feel so beautiful now that I am out of my old lady shoes."

The next day Barb and Vicki took Maggie shopping for her Maid of Honour dress. They showed her the dress that Vicki would be wearing so Maggie could choose a complimentary colour. She chose a pink, loose-fitting dress with a V-neckline to match Vicki's dress. She also picked beige pumps. She looked lovely in her dress and Vicki was so proud of her sister.

CHAPTER 53

TRIP TO NIAGARA FALLS

Following a very busy week of shopping and wedding plans, Tom and Vicki decided to go to Niagara Falls for a weekend to relax. They were both very wound up with the excitement and tired from the shopping. Tom and his groomsmen had also been out selecting their trousers, shirts, and shoes. Tom bought silver pens engraved with the date of the wedding for his groomsmen, Martin and Charlie. Vicki bought an eighteen inch gold chain for Maggie to wear with her dress.

Tom and Vicki booked a lovely room overlooking the falls. The room had a king sized bed and there was a Jacuzzi in the room as well. There was a couch, a desk in front of the window, two chairs and a dresser with a flat screen television mounted on the wall above it.

The view from the window was spectacular. Their room was facing both falls; the Canadian Horseshoe Falls and the American Falls. They were both beautiful. "What a natural wonder," thought Vicki. When Tom and Vicki arrived, they went for a swim in the large indoor pool. Vicki had just bought a new bathing suit for their trip to Hawaii and she was anxious to try it out. This was her first tankini, turquoise blue and purple. Tom thought she looked wonderful; he kept calling her sexy so she felt wonderful and sexy. After swimming, they spent fifteen minutes in the whirlpool; it was hot and made them sleepy. They went up to their room for an hour's rest. When they awoke they were in each other's arms wearing nothing but their underwear. Tom felt so warm; his skin was soft and Vicki felt she never wanted to leave his embrace.

"My Dear, will you join me in the walk-in shower?" whispered Tom.

"I would love to; be right there."

Vicki had packed, in her suitcase, her own liquid shower gel, Japanese Cherry Blossom, as it was a scent that they both loved. Tom rubbed gel on Vicki's shoulders. Then he traced circles around her back with the bubbles.

"Oh Honey, that smells so good."

Then his hands slid down to encompass her bottom. He gave a little squeeze and she giggled. He then, very gently turned her around to face him. The water from the shower was hitting his head and splashing on Vicki's face and she had to close her eyes. She could feel Tom putting gel on her shoulders and working his way down to her breasts. He was very gentle and it felt very slippery but wonderful. As his fingers reached her tummy she started to laugh.

"That tickles."

"Good, it's supposed to make you happy."

"Oh! How sensual this feels."

Now it was Vicki's turn to give pleasure to Tom. She rubbed the gel on his back and shoulders, gently massaging his skin as she worked her way down to his taut buttocks.

"Turn around," Vicki whispered and he turned slowly to face her. He looked like a Greek God and Vicki loved every inch of him.

"Your body is so beautiful, my love."

"Not as beautiful as yours, kitten."

Vicki squeezed the shower gel onto Tom's shoulders and rubbed it until bubbles formed. Then she massaged the bubbles all over his muscular chest, and down his abdomen to the loveliest erection Vicki had ever seen.

"Just put on a robe and I will carry you to paradise, my Dear," Tom whispered.

"Oh how wonderful you are." she sighed.

Their bodies were still wet from the shower as they hugged and kissed and Vicki could feel his desire hard against her thigh. It wasn't long before they were together as one.

"Tom, I love you so much."

"And I love you and I can't wait to make you my wife."

They walked from the hotel to Fallsview Casino for their buffet dinner and then a few hours of fun at the slots. Vicki liked the new automated roulette game as she could play for just $20.00. It was 11:45 when they returned to their room and they were both quite tired. Tom poured 2 glasses of wine and they sat on the bed sipping wine and watching a little television.

Next morning they visited the Butterfly Conservatory. They strolled through the building that housed all the butterflies. As Tom and Vicki walked and admired the beauty of the butterflies, some of them flew up to them and landed on their arms, hands, head or shoulders. What a thrill this was!

"Oh Tom, just look at this lovely Monarch butterfly. It came right over to me and landed on my hand. Isn't it pretty?"

"It is absolutely gorgeous, one of God's miracles."

Then they went outside and walked through the grounds to admire the outstanding flowers, plants, trees and ornaments.

"Tom, could you please stand by the statue over there so I can take your picture?"

"Sure, Dear, then I will take yours."

Vicki hadn't packed her regular camera with the ten second delay; instead she had her small camera because she could carry it in her purse.

As Tom was positioning himself for the picture, another couple came along.

"Why don't you both get in the picture and I will take it for you," the girl offered.

"Thank you and we will do the same for you," said Vicki.

Now they had a nice picture with both of them in it.

After a day in the fresh air Tom and Vicki were both starving and decided that a steak sounded like a good idea. They went for a great steak dinner with baked potato, seasonal vegetables, a glass of Merlot and they finished off with a cup of coffee. Then they took a long walk marvelling at the beauty of the falls.

Next morning Tom and Vicki headed home so Tom could prepare for work the next day. They both agreed they were much more relaxed after their weekend away.

CHAPTER 54

THE WEDDING

Soon it was time for all twenty-four travellers to meet at the airport for their trip to Hawaii. This trip took twelve hours as they had to switch planes in Vancouver. They were all carrying garment bags and pulling suitcases. It took a while to check everyone in and send them to the departure gate which Vicki was so happy to be able to walk to.

They stopped at a coffee shop for something to drink before boarding the plane.

"I absolutely love this coffee." Vicki ordered a latte and enjoyed every sip.

The movies on the plane were Shrek and Shrek ll so the teenagers were all happy. The adults had books to read but with all the activity on the plane such as food, Duty Free sales, handing out headsets and pillows, then blankets, there was not a lot of time to read. They were able to get a little sleep on the trip. They were in Hawaii before they knew it. Vicki could hardly contain herself.

"I am getting married to the most wonderful man in the world and "Thank God—I am healthy."

When they arrived at the resort and spa they were all so tired that they decided to have something to eat and then go to their rooms to rest. The next day would be a busy day as it was the day of the wedding.

The next morning the sun was shining in the window and it woke Tom and Vicki up early. The birds were singing and when Vicki looked out the window she could see green grass and flowers, and she remembered they were in Hawaii. They showered and dressed, then went downstairs for breakfast and to meet their families and friends. All the ladies had spa appointments for a mani/pedi, then hair appointments. Since Vicki's hair was short, she had it curled and the hairdresser put flowers in each curl. She was not wearing a veil. Maggie had long hair so she had it in an upsweep on top of her head with flowers, as well, in the back. She looked marvelous.

The wedding was at four o'clock at a Chapel on the hotel grounds. This was a small chapel, all white walls and seats. There were gardenias and honeysuckle adorning the walls and the altar. There was a pink ribbon tied in a bow on each chair in the chapel.

"What a lovely picture."

There was a red carpet down the middle aisle and white carpets at the front. They all met at the chapel at three thirty.

"What a nice surprise."

Two beautiful, young women wearing grass skirts greeted them at the door and placed a flower lei of pink and white around each person's neck as they entered the chapel. The girls were very friendly. They even did a little hula dance. Vicki smiled and said:

"Thank you."

Then she proceeded into the chapel where she was about to marry the love of her life. Vicki could hardly contain her excitement. This was the best day of her life and she wanted to make Tom very happy too.

The wedding was beautiful; better than Vicki could ever have imagined. Tom and his brother Martin stood in anticipation at the front of the chapel. They were both dressed in white trousers and pale blue shirts, open at the neck. Now Vicki had two very handsome men standing and waiting for her. She felt so privileged. Tom looked absolutely perfect and Vicki wondered how she could be so lucky to be able to spend the rest of her days and nights with this man.

"Oh! Those nights, can't wait."

The music started. It was Andrea Bocelli's *Can't Help Falling In Love.* Maggie started very slowly down the aisle. She looked beautiful in her loose-fitting pink dress. She carried a lovely white orchid. When Maggie reached the front of the chapel it was Vicki's turn. She was excited to finally be marrying the love of her life. Charlie walked her down the aisle. He was wearing white trousers and a pale blue shirt that matched Tom and Martin's. As they began their walk, Vicki took Charlie's arm but this time it was not to stabilize her or help her walk. Vicki was so proud of her wonderful son and she knew he and Annie were happy for her as she was marrying the man of her dreams and best of all, *in good health*. As Vicki and Charlie neared the front of the chapel, Tom turned to face them. Vicki and Tom's eyes met and she thought she would pass out, he was so gorgeous.

The minister approached them and read a passage from the Bible. 1 Corinthians 13:

Love is patient, love is kind. It does not envy, it does not boast, it is not proud.

When the minister had finished reading the whole passage he turned to Vicki and Tom and asked them to join hands and they exchanged rings. When the minister said:

"I now pronounce you husband and wife," the tears started to roll down Vicki's cheeks. She was happier in this moment than she had ever been before.

"Now I am Mrs. Thomas Harrison."

CHAPTER 55

THE WEDDING RECEPTION

The reception followed outside at the Wedding Centre also on the hotel grounds. Everyone kicked off their shoes in order to walk in the sand. Tom and Vicki and Maggie and Martin formed the receiving line and the guests took their seats at the tables, which had been placed on the beach in a horseshoe fashion to allow for conversation.

The table linens were all white and there were white and pink orchids in hand-made bamboo vases about eighteen inches apart all around the tables. The dinner consisted of roasted pig which was cooked on the beach, on a spit. There was an apple in the pig's mouth and the spit turned slowly to cook the meat. There was a delicious Waldorf salad, Hawaiian coconut rice and Mahi Mahi with brown sugar Soy glaze. Before the dinner was served they all shared Hawaiian mango bread and a Pina Colada. A fancy fresh fruit salad followed the meal.

Then the wedding cake was brought to the table. It was white cake with pink icing and several different coloured flowers cascading down the side of the cake. The flowers were real and had been dipped in sugar. This made a fantastic looking cake. The whole meal was delicious.

After dinner, Maggie spoke first and toasted the Bride and Groom. Then Martin told a few silly stories about his older brother, Tom.

While everyone waited for the tables to be cleared and the music to start, the two young ladies who had previously been at the chapel, gave a demonstration of hula dancing. Vicki and several of her guests got up to try this dance. It was a lot of fun and Vicki was so happy to be dancing again.

After the tables were cleared, the hotel provided a disc jockey who set up on the beach. This D.J. had a wide range of music taped and everyone danced. Vicki was thrilled to be able to dance at last. It was wonderful, especially for Vicki as she was finally able to dance all night. They danced and danced and danced. Vicki didn't want to sit down. *"I feel normal at last."*

CHAPTER 56

THE HONEYMOON

On Sunday they just rested by the multi-level pool and they swam together.

"Would you like to go for couples Lomi Lomi massage, Tom? I understand it is very relaxing. You can have a traditional massage if you wish but I think I would like to try the hot stones with my massage. I have always wondered what it would be like."

"Sure, I have never had a massage before, but if we go together I will try it."

"Okay, I will book it for this afternoon."

They both enjoyed a massage with hot stones that took more than an hour. Since they had been in the sun all morning, they went to the bar for a cold drink and then to their room for a short nap. There was a luau on the beach with a variety show afterwards in the outside theatre that they wanted to attend.

The next day they planned to take a helicopter ride from their resort over a volcano and then past a waterfall.

"I am a little frightened Tom; I have never been in a helicopter before."

"Don't worry, it is a comfortable ride and I will be right beside you, holding your hand."

"Okay, I really want to do it, so let's go."

"The view from up here is sensational Tom. This is the first time I have seen an active volcano and it is unbelievable. Thanks for bringing me up here."

The next day they rented bikes from a local bike shop and they cycled along Alii Drive. The scenery was superb.

On day four Tom and Vicki rested on the beach and at the pool.

On day five they went to Kealakekua Bay to swim with the dolphins. This was a lot of fun. One dolphin kissed Vicki and Tom got a picture of it.

They returned to their resort by about three o'clock. They had to have a short nap as they were going to view the Manta Ray and then have a sunset dinner at Ray on the Bay. This would be a very full day.

Day six was their last day in Hawaii and they spent it walking on the beach gathering shells and stones to take back home with them. They went for a long swim in the pool and then dressed for dinner and a show on the Hawaii Lawn.

Vicki and Tom made love at least once a day and Vicki felt wonderful and so happy.

It was a dream honeymoon.

CHAPTER 57

AFTER THE HONEYMOON

When they got back home, Vicki sold her condo and moved into Tom's house.

One day, about a week after they returned from their honeymoon, Tom was at the bank and he overheard one of his long-time customers asking the tellers if they knew anyone who would like a cat. The customer was moving to an apartment and animals were not allowed.

Tom approached her and asked:

"How old is the cat?"

"She is about three years old and she has been spayed but not de-clawed. She is very friendly and loves to be patted."

"My wife and I have been thinking about getting a cat. Could we meet her and see if she likes us?"

"Of course, how wonderful. How about tomorrow evening?"

"I'm sure that will be fine. Is seven o'clock okay for you?"

"Yes, I look forward to your visit."

When Tom arrived home, Vicki was preparing dinner. He kissed her and said:

"I have a surprise for you Dear."

"Give me a hint."

"Okay but just one small hint:" "Meow."

"You have a cat?"

"Not quite yet but we have an appointment to meet her tomorrow evening."

Tom explained the situation to Vicki and she was so excited that she hardly slept all night.

The next evening they visited Tom's customer and the cat just loved both of them, climbing on their knees and purring. They were pleased to take her and it made Tom's customer extremely happy and relieved to have a good home for her cat.

This little cat was a pretty calico cat named Cali.

Tom and Vicki spent the next few months getting used to being married and awaiting the arrival of Vicki's first grandchild.

AUTHOR'S NOTES

NORMAL PRESSURE HYDROCEPHALUS (NPH)

WHAT ARE THE SYMPTOMS OF NPH?

The most visible and recognizable sign of NPH is difficulty walking-Gait Disturbance

This is often followed by confusion and memory loss-Cognitive Impairment

The third symptom is trouble controlling your bladder-Urinary Incontinence

CAUSES

Any condition that blocks the flow of CSF cerebrospinal fluid

No known reason

EXAMS AND TESTS

Test walking (gait) changes

Lumbar puncture is sometimes used to test gait changes, before and after the LP test.

Head CT or MRI

TREATMENT

The treatment of choice is surgery to place a tube called a shunt into the brain. The ventricular end of the shunt is passed through the brain and into the lateral ventricle. This tube re-routes the excess CSF to the abdomen

To see the full article go to: normal pressure hydrocephalus medlinplus

TREATMENT 2

There is a surgical procedure called endoscopic third ventriculostomy which eliminates the need for a shunt

Please see: endoscopic third ventriculostomy

For further information you may contact:

Spina Bifida & Hydrocephalus Association of Canada

Tel. 1-800-565-9488   www.sbhac.ca

Edwards Brothers Malloy
Thorofare, NJ USA
January 20, 2014